CW00863487

THE VIADUCT CUP

THE ALLSORTS FC SERIES: BOOK 1

NIC CLARE

FAR LANDS PRESS

ALSO BY NIC CLARE

The Allsorts FC Series

Book One: The Viaduct Cup

Book Two: The Search

Book Three: The Telegram

First published in 2022 in Great Britain by

Far Lands Press
www.nicclare.com
© Nic Clare

ISBN: 978-1-7396017-0-6

PROLOGUE

The Nether Bridge Chronicle

Excitement is building in anticipation of the 1913 Viaduct Cup final on Saturday next. Holders Carmody Mill travel to the Sidings football ground in Nether Bridge to take on underdogs Bamford Hatworks. The Hatters are striving to win for the first time in their long history while the visitors will play for their twelfth consecutive title. Fans of the beautiful game shouldn't miss out on what has been billed the match of the decade. Old rivalries live long and Bamford Hatworks Football Club will throw everything they have at the accomplished Carmody team in an attempt to steal a famous victory. There is no doubt the match will be a hard fought affair. Kick off is at 3.15pm.

CHAPTER 1

The football landed on a crate of tomatoes with a satisfying splat.

"What on earth…!" The market stall holder picked up the ball. "Who kicked this?" she said wiping the red pulp from her eyes.

I would have made a run for it, but she had my best ball. "Sorry Mrs Finch!" I said. "It was an accident." I took the scuffed leather football from her and with a strong right boot launched it down the steps into the cobbled market square. As I set off after it, skipping down the steps two at a time, Mrs Finch called out after me,

"Get back here Kit Bracken! You owe me for these tomatoes!"

I weaved through the crush of market day shoppers with the ball at my feet. As I side-stepped a pile of horse manure, I bashed into a woman who dropped her shopping basket.

"Mind out!" she said as she gathered herself. "Young ladies should not be running about the streets with footballs."

"Sorry!" I said, not sorry at all as the ball bounced ahead of me. I leapt forward, trapped it beneath my foot, then turned to block a man in a smart suit as he reached out for my coat.

"Apologise at once!" he said, but I was away. "Disgraceful behaviour," he muttered as he helped the woman with her shopping.

I could hear the rattled crowd behind me, the shouts of disapproval and the crash of boxes falling from the market stalls. As I dribbled the ball through the crowd, I imagined myself on a real football pitch. The disgruntled shoppers were the desperate opposition defence. I passed one, then left the next in my wake. The third, an old street sweeper, stood his ground, but I feigned a kick to the right and slotted the ball through his legs. I looked up, jumped over a beer barrel, and neared my target. Sergeant Beswick had his back to me, he was busy herding the match day crowds. I booted the ball straight at him. His helmet almost fell off as he stumbled forward. I didn't hang around.

"Oi! I ought to burst that ball," he shouted. "You're causing a public nuisance."

"Afternoon Sergeant." I picked up the ball. "I'd stay and chat but I've got somewhere to be." I laughed as I ran backwards, but pulled up short as the tram rang its bell and trundled through the square. Passengers jumped off as it slowed. A poster on the side advertised the 1913 Viaduct Cup final, Bamford Hatworks versus Carmody Mill, Saturday at 3pm. The town hall clock struck two. It was almost time.

CHAPTER 2

I nipped down a side alley and headed towards the Sidings football ground, the home of the Bamford Hatworks football team. A train blew its whistle in support as it thundered over the huge red brick railway viaduct that has always watched over our town of Nether Bridge. The steam from the train joined with the smoke from the factory chimneys and drifted through the rows of back to back terraced houses, along the ginnels and past the heaving corner pubs. I joined the crowds spilling from the railway station; they were in full voice. An electric excitement crackled in the air. No one was more excited than me. No one could be prouder. The captain of the Bamford Hatworks football team was my big brother, Bernie Bracken.

They had a chance at victory. Imagine that? Bamford Hatworks football team, winners of the Viaduct Cup. It was Bernie's one and only dream, and I had been there with him every kick of the way, training with him, tackling him, kicking long balls for him to control, guarding the goal while he took penalties. So it was my dream too - for Bernie to win the Viaduct Cup - for a Bracken to win the Viaduct Cup.

I picked up the ball, elbowed my way through the crowd and took a handbill from a group of suffragettes taking advantage of the turnout. A speaker stood on an empty fruit and veg cart shouting through a loud hailer,

"..to join the great pilgrimage to London. We will march together and congregate in a rally in Hyde Park. They cannot ignore our numbers. Who is with me?"

A cheer went up, and the singing started;

"Shout, shout, up with your song, cry with the wind, for the dawn is breaking."

I joined in. Why should men have the vote and not women? Perhaps if women could vote like the men, we might be allowed to play football like them too. Now, there's a cause worth fighting for.

I carried on singing to myself as I left the rally

and neared the football ground, "March, march—many as one, shoulder to shoulder and friend to friend."

A visiting fair had set up their attractions in the street outside the turnstiles. There was hoopla and a coconut shy, toffee apples and an organ grinder with a monkey in a waistcoat, causing mischief. The silver band was playing hymns and hawkers were selling match day programmes, scarves and rattles. But the biggest attraction was at the end of the street. A group had formed a circle and were clapping and jeering. They had a football goal up against the wall and a large man in full kit and goal-keeping gloves was jumping up and down. I recognised him straight away, Len Murgotroyd. He was the best goalkeeper of his day, he famously went three whole seasons without conceding a goal.

"Fancy your chances, miss?" A fairground man in a bowler hat was inviting people to step forward and take a shot against Len. "Do you think you can get one past the great Len Murgotroyd? Step up. A penny a penalty. Win yourself a medal. Tell the world you scored against the greatest." He held up a silver medal on a ribbon. A young lad, egged on by his pals, stepped out of the crowd and peeled off his jacket.

"I'll take him on," he smiled.

"Good lad," the man said, handing over a football. "Get ready, Len," he called back, "we've got a lively one here."

Len pumped his hands together and raised his arms to fill the goalmouth. He was huge. The lad took a few short, deep breaths, placed the ball on the spot, and kicked it as hard as he was able. But Len was a match for him. He reached out and thumped the ball away. The crowd groaned, then clapped. The lad put his jacket on, grinning and shaking his head.

"Good effort, son. Good effort. Who's next? Who will take on the best?"

"I will." A voice came from the crowd opposite.

"Who said that?" The man held up his arm, scanning the rabble.

"I did," the voice said.

"Come on out, sir."

Along with everyone else, I stood on tiptoes to see who was willing to take on the challenge. I slunk back down when I saw my dad emerge from the crowd.

"What's your name, sir?"

"Stanley Bracken," Dad said. There was a murmur of excitement. I could tell from the colour of his cheeks that he'd been drinking. Something told me to leave, to spare myself the shame, but my feet were rooted to the spot.

The man in the bowler hat quietened the crowd. "Do you want to take on the great Len Murgotroyd, Mr Bracken?"

"The question is, does he want to take on the great Stanley Bracken?" Dad said, waving his hat drawing a round of applause. "You take my penny and I'll take that medal."

I closed my eyes. He was setting himself up to fail. Again. He took off his coat and rolled up his sleeves. Len Murgotroyd stepped forward to shake Dad's hand. "I remember you. You played for Bamford Hatworks back in my day."

"That's right," Dad said, smiling at his notoriety.

"Well, you never got one past me then, and you won't get one past me now," he raised a cheer and went back to his goalmouth.

The girl next to me clapped her hands and looked at me with a smile. "This'll be good."

I shook my head. "No one could score against that goalkeeper. Look at the size of him!"

"A lad did it earlier. Got himself a medal."

"It's impossible," I said, predicting my dad's failure.

"It's not easy, no, but it's not impossible. If it was easy, the medal wouldn't be worth anything, would it?"

Dad took his time placing the ball on the spot, then stepped back.

The man in the bowler hat raised his arms. "Lets have some quiet ladies and gentlemen. When you're ready, Mr Bracken."

CHAPTER 3

Dad hasn't always been an embarrassment. He was a special player as a young man, the best we ever had. He captained the Bamford Hatworks team all the way to the final of the Viaduct Cup. I'll never forget the day of the cup final. I was eight years old and my dad was the toast of the town. We were so proud, me and Mum and Bernie watching on from the stands as he walked on to the pitch in his green jersey. Football meant everything to Dad, so it meant everything to us, too. The day before the match, we went to find him down at the Sidings after school. He was always the first one to arrive at training and the last to leave, so we knew where to find him. We let him take penalties against us, both of us in goal guarding each post, but he still got the ball over the line. He could do anything, he was the strongest, fastest and smartest player on any football pitch. When a heavy rain shower came in over the viaduct, we ran and took shelter under one of the empty arches. Crouched down with the ball at his feet, Dad wiped the rain from his hair and smiled. "This time tomorrow this place will be filled with crowds cheering us on."

"Are you nervous about tomorrow, Dad?" I asked.

"Nervous?" He shook his head. "I'm not nervous, I'm ready. In this town there is no greater honour than to lift the Viaduct Cup."

"Why?" Bernie asked. "Why does it mean so much?" I shook my head at him. If he didn't understand now, then he never would. Dad put his hand on Bernie's shoulder and looked back out onto the field as the rain dripped down from the shrubs growing out of the brickwork of the viaduct.

"It's about honour and pride and tradition. It has a long history. They played the first ever Viaduct Cup match in 1870. That was between Carmody Cottonworks and Bamford Hatters as well."

"They both made the final then too?" I asked.

"They were the only two teams. If you want to understand why the Viaduct Cup means so much, you have to understand the history. You know what happened in the 1860s, don't you?"

"Is that when you were born, Dad?" Bernie said with a smile.

"Oi! I'm not that old!" he laughed. "In the 1860s, there was a civil war in America. It was the union states of the north versus some confederate states in the south. Do you know what they grew in the southern states of America?"

"Sugar?" I said, hoping I was right so I could impress Dad.

"Cotton," he answered, putting his hand on my head with a smile. "Raw cotton that the mills in this town needed to make their cloth. Well, the sale of the cotton was paying for all the soldiers and guns and bullets for the south, so the north blockaded the ports, cut off their trade, their supply of money. But of course that meant the boats filled with the cotton couldn't get to us. When they cut off the raw cotton supply, the looms in the mills stopped working. No work meant no money, no money meant no food."

"So what happened to the workers?" Bernie asked.

"Hundreds lost their jobs, their homes, they

went hungry. There was disease and starvation, many people died. Some masters did what they could to keep their workforce going, others weren't so considerate."

"Don't tell me," Bernie shook his head. "Lord Carmody wasn't on the side of his workers."

"Well, it was the current Lord Carmody's father back then, but no, he wasn't. He closed his mill and laid everyone off. My mother and father amongst them."

"What about Mr Bamford? Did he lay his workers off too?"

Dad laughed. "Mr Bamford wasn't the Mr Bamford we know today. He was a young man, plain old Eli Bamford, foreman at Carmody Mill."

"He worked at Carmody Mill?" The two old men were such rivals I couldn't imagine Mr Bamford having anything at all to do with Lord Carmody.

"Mr Bamford began work at five years old, scavenging barefoot under the looms for loose cotton. But he was a bright lad and by the time he was fifteen he was a foreman."

"So how did he end up as the master at the hatworks?" Bernie asked.

"Have I never told you this story before?" Dad

shook his head at our ignorance. "Well, Bamford was laid off too, but he wasn't one to lie down without a fight, so he came up with a plan. He persuaded some local businessmen to back his idea of a hat factory. They didn't need cotton to make hats. He employed half the laid off Carmody workers to build the hatworks and provided employment. Bamford saved lives and showed Carmody up for the money obsessed toff he was. Carmody could have done more to help his workers, he should have done more. There was a lot of bitterness about that, between those who stayed with Carmody and those who went with Bamford. When the war was over and Carmody Mill started up again, the workers from each mill would fight out their rivalry. Your grandad was involved in all that. Brawling in the streets. In the end, the two masters were told by the mayor to sort it out. That's when they came up with the football match. A team from each mill would compete against one another. In time, other teams joined in and they named the competition the Viaduct Cup."

I nodded. "That's why it's so important for Mr Bamford to win the trophy. Because he's never won it before," I explained to Bernie as if I had always known the story.

"Until tomorrow," Dad winked. "Tomorrow, everything will change for us. I'll make sure of it."

CHAPTER 4

He was right about that. Everything did change after the match, but not in the way we hoped. With fifteen minutes to the final whistle, the Bamford boys were on the up. The equaliser went in off Dad's boot with such force that the ball flew through the back of the net and into the crowd. Having been two-nil down at halftime, the lads had achieved the impossible and clawed themselves back into the game. Dad scored again with minutes left on the clock. The Viaduct Cup was within reach. For the first time, the team no one believed in would sweep aside the favourites and make history. I could already sense the pride welling in my chest. I had a vision of Dad holding the trophy, his teammates all around him, the crowd roaring with joy. But it wasn't over. The teams were evenly matched and tired legs on both sides were slowing the pace. It happened all of a sudden, but slowly at the same time. Dad was pressing forward, the ball at his feet, when a Carmody defender flew in and kicked the ball away towards the Bamford net. Dad had to back-track. The Bamford goalkeeper crouched, ready to block the shot. They had caught our defence napping and there was no one to stop the attack. Dad lunged in with his studs in the air, the Carmody striker jumped out of the way, but Dad's leg jarred in the grass and he let out a terrific scream. The entire crowd drew in their breath at the crunching sound, but then there was silence for what felt like minutes. The Carmody forward netted the ball, but no one celebrated his goal. Everyone was waiting to see if Dad would get up, but he wasn't able. He writhed around on the grass and when the Bamford goalie ran over to check on him, he put his hand to his mouth and called for help. I knew it was bad from the look on Mum's face. "Wait here," she said as she pushed along the line in the terraces and made her way onto the pitch. The players surrounded Dad, shielding him from view, then the referee blew his whistle and waved the manager on from the sidelines.

A man behind us tutted. "Damned fool. That's his footballing days over."

We watched as they carried Dad off the pitch on a stretcher. His face was pale and scrunched up with pain, his leg was in an unnatural position and as careful as they were, every movement was agony. They took him straight home and laid him on the table in the front parlour. Mum set about boiling water and collecting clean towels. They sent Bernie to fetch the doctor and I sat beside Dad, wiping his forehead with a wet cloth. The pain sent him delirious, he was gripping at the table and grinding his teeth, the sweat was pouring off him. I just wanted it to stop, for him to fall asleep, I wanted to take the pain away for him, but it went on and on. An hour after we arrived home, some of the Bamford team looked in to check on Dad.

"What was the score?" Dad hauled himself onto his elbows when he saw them in the doorway.

"We lost five-three. I'm sorry Stan. We tried our best, but with their extra man they overran us."

Dad lay back and let out a frightening roar, like a wounded animal. I don't know if it was a roar of pain, anger, or disappointment. Perhaps it was a mixture of all three. When the doctor finally arrived, he gave Dad a shot of morphine and he fell into a fitful, fevered sleep.

"It's a bad break Mrs Bracken," he explained to Mum in the kitchen. "If he survives the next twenty-four hours, he should live."

"Will he walk?"

"In time he might, but never without pain, never without a stick."

CHAPTER 5

Dad lived, of course, but it wasn't the life he wanted. It took months for him to recover his general health. The leg healed, but the doctor was right when he said Dad would never walk properly again. He was so long away from the hatworks that they gave his job to someone else. Maybe he could have accepted that his footballing career was over if he had lifted the cup just once. But it wasn't to be and he let the disappointment, the failure, eat away at him. He started drinking to mask the pain in his leg at first, but it wasn't long before the drink became more of a problem than the leg. It was through the fog of drink that he started looking for someone to blame.

"It was a bad tackle. A dirty tackle. They knew I

was the best player and they came after me," he said for the hundredth time as we sat down for tea.

"I've told you before, Stan," Mum said as she dished out the watery stew and wrinkled potatoes. "It wasn't a tackle. It was just bad luck."

"What do you know about it?" Dad said, gripping his spoon. "You weren't even there."

"I was there! I saw it all happen in front of me."

"You weren't on the pitch though, were you? They were a filthy team. Hacking at me for the whole match. They were never going to let me win that game and they'd do anything to beat me down."

"You have to stop this Stan," Mum said, sitting at the table.

"You know why, don't you? Because I'm a Bracken, I'm Den Bracken's son and no one will ever let me forget it."

"Oh, Stan!" Mum put her head in her hands.

"It's true. You were there Bernie? Kit? You saw what happened? I was a target, and they didn't miss." He took a spoonful of the stew and spat it out. "What is this?"

"It's the best I can do on one wage after you've taken half of my pay packet to the pub."

"I don't want to drink, but it's the only thing

that helps my leg. We can't afford the medicine. What do you expect me to do?"

Mum gestured for me and Bernie to leave, so we took our bowls of stew and went to sit on the stairs.

"I need you to find work, Stan," Mum said, lowering her voice. "I can't do this on my own. We were always a team, you, me, Bernie and Kit. It's like we're a player down. We need you back on the pitch. We need you to contribute."

"I can't play. I'm injured," Dad said, raising his voice. We heard the scrape of the chair on the stone kitchen floor as he stood. "I'm permanently injured. I'm a cripple. No one will give me work."

"Someone will. Stan, you have to try. We're three months behind on the rent already. We can't go on like this."

"I am trying! No one will have me."

"What about the rag and bone round? Old George said he'd let you take that on. He wants to retire, it's perfect. Bernie will help you with the horse."

"You're not listening to me!" he shouted. His chair clattered as it fell backwards. "I don't need to hear this in my own home. I'm the man of this house. You don't tell me what to do."

"I'm not telling you what to do," Mum called out after Dad, who slammed the kitchen door on his way out. "I'm just trying to keep us together," she said to herself quietly.

CHAPTER 6

Dad didn't come home until the early hours. I woke to find him kneeling at Bernie's bedside, shaking him awake.

"Dad?" I sat up and rubbed my eyes.

"Come on, get up. Both of you. I want to show you something."

We dressed quickly and followed Dad outside. He didn't speak as we followed him through the empty streets. It was a warm summer's night and the dawn light was blue in the sky. He took us back to the pitch at the Sidings and sat down against the goalpost, stretching out his bad leg in front of him, resting his stick on the grass. He took a bottle of beer from his inside pocket, pulled out the cork with his teeth and spat it into the goalmouth. Me and

Bernie looked at each other, confused and still half asleep, then sat down next to him.

"You never met my Dad did you? Your grandfather?" Dad said as he took a swig of the beer.

"He died before we came along," Bernie answered.

"He was born down there, did you know that?" He pointed towards the river.

"He was born on the river? On a boat, you mean?" I asked.

"There are caves on the river bank, carved into the sandstone. His father was a navvy. He worked on the railways. He came to Nether Bridge to build the viaduct. Some families lived in the caves. When the viaduct was complete, they got work in the cotton mills." We looked up as an early train trundled over the viaduct. "He was a rogue, my old dad. Den was his name. He spent more time in prison than he did out."

"Prison? What for?" Bernie asked, wide eyed.

"He was a notorious housebreaker. I used to go with him, when I was small."

"You did?" I couldn't imagine my dad breaking the law. He would never do anything that might affect his chances of playing football.

"I didn't want to, but he was my dad and I was

hungry. I'd go in through the coal hole or a small window at the back of the houses and let him in. Then I'd wait outside on watch while he went inside and took what he could."

"You were a burglar?" A tone of disappointment crept into Bernie's voice. He had always looked up to Dad, but ever since the accident, the gloss of his image was beginning to tarnish.

"Not me. My dad. I didn't have a choice, did I?"

"Why was he a thief? Couldn't he find a job?" I asked.

"There was no work. Not back then. I told you about this," he said, frustrated at my question, "because of the civil war in America."

"You said that he lost his job in the cotton famine, but you didn't say he was a thief! You didn't say he stole from others," Bernie shook his head.

"I don't think you can judge him, son, not unless you know what it's like to starve like that. Besides, he only took from the big houses, those who could afford to keep food on their tables. There are some families who did well out of the cotton famine, those who increased their prices, those who could lie low until it was all over."

"The rich you mean?" I asked.

"Well, if they weren't rich before the famine, they were afterwards."

"People like Lord Carmody." I nodded in understanding.

Bernie didn't understand. "But you said that Mr Bamford started the hatworks and gave people jobs. Didn't your dad get a job with him?"

"No, by the time that came about, it was too late. Dad had spent time inside and no one would employ him. Once he'd been to prison, no one would give him a go, so it just went on and on. He had no choice but to become a crook. I can only have been four or five when I went with him the first time."

"But you stopped though, didn't you, Dad? When you were old enough to know better?" Bernie asked, still struggling to believe what he was hearing.

"Of course. I didn't want a life of crime. I turned my life around. I did that. No one else. Me," he gritted his teeth and pointed to his chest with the bottle. "When I was fifteen, Dad got sent down for a long stretch, so I made a break for it. I got myself a job at the hatworks. It was the best thing I ever did. That's where I met your mother. She was working in the cutting room. I bowled her over with my skills on the football pitch." He laughed at the memory. "I promised your mother I'd win the Viaduct Cup for her. I promised her I would be a Bracken she could be proud of, not another Bracken to cross the street to avoid. The thing is, my old dad left a legacy when he died."

"What kind of legacy?" Bernie asked.

"A bad one. His name, our name, Bracken. A Bracken in this town is no good. Doesn't matter what we do, we'll always be Brackens. Worthless. No one will ever give us a chance. I've spent my life trying to change that legacy. I thought I could do it through football. I thought I could be Stan Bracken, winner of the Viaduct Cup, not Stan Bracken, son of that old lag Den. And I almost did it," he looked down and shook his head. "I would have done it. I could have won the cup, but this town wouldn't let that happen. Look at the state of me now, look what they've done to me."

I shuffled my legs underneath me; the dew was seeping through my coat. I wanted to reach out and give Dad a hug; he looked so sad. But he was drunk, and I was a little frightened of what he might do.

Dad took another swig of his beer. "I nearly did it," he said to himself. "I was so close." Bernie was quiet. Dad grabbed his knee as a bolt of pain shot through it, and he scrunched up his face, then he drained the beer bottle as if it were a medicine that would take away the agony. He looked at the bottle, surprised that it was already empty, threw it away into the darkness, then reached out for Bernie. "It's up to you now, son," he said.

"Me?" Bernie kneeled in front of him.

"It's a son's job to better his father. I almost did it. I almost won the cup and wiped out Dad's legacy. Now you need to finish it."

The blood drained from Bernie's face. "But Dad, I'm still at school."

"I know. I know. It'll take time and that's alright. You need to train hard, you need to grow, get stronger. When the time comes, you'll start work at the hatworks and then you can join the team. It's your job now, son. It's your job to win the Viaduct Cup and save the family name."

CHAPTER 7

It took a while for Mum's pleas to filter through to Dad and after a few lean months, he pulled himself together. I was on my way to the park with the football at my feet when Dad pulled up next to me on the horse and cart. He'd found some energy to get up and bring home some money using the rag and bone round. Gulliver, the old nag, was a plodder of a horse, especially when pulling a load, and he used the excuse of seeing me to stop and say hello. I stroked his mane and let him nuzzle my hand. Dad sat on the cart holding the reins. The flat trailer behind was piled with scrap metal, bags of old clothes and worn out items no one wanted.

"Can I give you a lift, m'lady?" Dad smiled,

gesturing to the seat beside him. He was in good spirits and I thought perhaps he had made a change. A wave of hope rushed through me. Finally things could get back to normal. I jumped up beside him and he sent Gulliver on his way. Dad was sober. His eyes were clear and his cheeks had little nicks of dried blood on them where he had attempted to shave.

I looked up at him and smiled at his cheery mood. "Have you collected much stuff?" I asked.

Dad shrugged. "Not much, but then a rag round will never make us rich, will it? RAG BONE!" he shouted as we turned on to the street by the river. "I hope you're helping Bernie with his football?" he asked, nodding to the ball on my lap.

"Of course I am. When he comes to the park, I let him take shots against me."

"That lad needs to focus more. He's got a natural talent, he musn't waste it."

"He does focus," I said in Bernie's defence.

"If he wants to be the best, he should train more. He should follow your example." I smiled at the compliment.

We slowed as a woman came out of her back-yard and waved to say she had something for us.

"Mum must be happy," I said. "That you're bringing home some money."

"It's not enough, though. I'm the man of the house, the breadwinner. It's not right that she brings in more than I do."

"But that's not your fault though, is it? If it wasn't for your leg…"

"No, you're right. It's not my fault. I'm owed better than this," he squeezed his knee and reminded himself of the accident. The woman appeared with a sack of old rags.

"Can you do anything with these?" she said, holding up the bag.

"Sling them on the back, Mrs Butterworth."

She nodded and threw the bag onto the cart. Dad geed Gulliver on and we turned towards the nicer part of town, to the three-storey houses overlooking the park. Dad sat up straight and began looking down the alleyways as we passed, then he pulled up and looking around the empty street, he slid down from the cart.

"Wait here a minute," he said as he picked up his stick and limped down the lane. I watched him go, but intrigued, I jumped down and followed him thinking he he might need help carrying the scrap. I found him in the back garden of a large house, peering in through the window of a wooden shed. He moved quietly, looking around him as he went. He tried the shed door, but it was locked, so he used his elbow to break the glass of the window. I felt a sharp intake of breath stab me in the heart as I realised what he was doing. He was stealing, breaking into the shed. He reached in and pulled out an old carriage clock. It looked like it was being repaired, but it was nice, with a gold-coloured face and polished wood. Dad slipped it under his coat and then walked back towards the street and the waiting cart. He saw me watching and stopped dead in his tracks. We held eye contact for a moment before we heard a dog barking down the lane, so we rushed back to the cart. Dad put the clock in the bag of rags and set Gully on his way. We sat in silence for at least three streets. The only words were the shouts of 'Rag Bone' as we entered a new road.

"I don't make enough on the rag and bone round," Dad said finally. "And it's not like I take from anyone who will miss it. It's just scrap to them, but to us it's rent. It's nothing to them, but every-thing to us."

"But what if you get caught?" I asked.

"I won't. I don't do it all the time. This town

owes us and it's only fair that we take it. It's not like I want to. If things were fair, we wouldn't be in this position."

I couldn't help but agree with him. Why should people live in big houses without a care in the world, while we struggled to put food on the table? It was simply about making the world a fairer place. We pulled up next to a house in the middle of a spring clean. All the windows and doors were open, and the curtains billowed in the breeze. We could see a pair of silver candlesticks on the table from the height of our cart.

"Stay here," Dad said as he slipped from his seat. He was quite nimble when he wanted to be, hopping with his bad leg in the air to speed towards the open door. He stopped at the house and called out.

"Any scrap?" There was no answer, so he went inside and grabbed the candlesticks. On his way out, he spotted something else, a vase or a jug of some sort. He reached for it and dropped one of the candlesticks. I didn't hear anything, but I saw Dad look back as if he had been disturbed, so I leapt down and ran to help. I grabbed the candlesticks so Dad could use his stick to rush back to the cart. We settled down and Gully walked on towards the scrap yard. Dad looked over and put his hand on my knee in thanks. I smiled at the thought of what we had done. It was thrilling, almost as good as playing football. My hands tingled and my heart thundered inside my chest.

"Your mother hears nothing of this," Dad said. I nodded. I knew it was wrong then, just as I know it is wrong now, but it was something that I shared with Dad. There was a hidden bond between us. Me and him alone, our secret.

CHAPTER 8

I went out with Dad on his rounds for six months or more before we got caught. I split my time between school, chores at home, playing football with Bernie, and helping Dad on his rounds. We fell into a silent routine. Neither of us spoke about what we were doing, but we both agreed that we weren't causing any harm. Not really. We were only taking from those who could bear the loss. The middle classes who had insurance and plenty of money. Those who probably wouldn't even notice anything was missing for weeks. I would walk on ahead of the cart and see what I could find. If I came across something small enough to take by myself, I would collect it and slip it onto the cart as Dad drove past. If there was something bigger, I would signal to Dad to stop and we would collect it together. I'll never forget the rush of excitement that went through me when I found some loot, the nod of approval when Dad agreed it was worth something. Dad sold the stolen goods on and came home with money in his pocket. I was contributing to my family, playing my part in keeping us together. I had a purpose. For the first time since the accident, things were looking up. But I suppose the good times for the Bracken family would never last.

Sergeant Beswick didn't wait to be invited in. He pushed Mum aside and one of his constables barged his way through and grabbed Dad before he could get away.

"What is this?" Mum said, still in her apron from cooking.

"Stanley Bracken, you're under arrest."

"What for?" Mum said, believing there had been a terrible mistake.

"Theft Mrs Bracken. I'm afraid rags and bones are not the only thing your husband has been collecting on his rounds."

"That's not true. Is it Stan?"

Dad lowered his head.

"Stan? Tell them it's not true."

Me and Bernie came in from the yard just as

the constable was leading Dad out in handcuffs. Mum grabbed hold of him and held him back. The constable let them have a moment.

"I'm sorry," Dad whispered.

"Come along now Mr Bracken. We can sort this out at the station."

"It's a mistake," Dad said loudly now. "Mind my leg!" he screamed as he was pulled away. "I'm not my father, but you'll never let me forget it, will you? A crime happens in this town and you immediately think of the Brackens. You ought to do your jobs properly. Go out and catch the real criminals, the masters fleecing their workers for every penny they can get."

"That's enough now Mr Bracken. You can tell us all about it at the police station."

Mum picked her coat off the hook in the hall to follow.

"No need for you to come with us, Mrs Bracken," Sergeant Beswick blocked her way. "Stan will be with us for some time."

"Do you have evidence?" Mum asked, her face flushed.

"We have a witness and we found quite a haul of stolen property in the scrap yard."

"A witness?" Things weren't looking good for

Dad. We watched as they bundled him, protesting all the way into the back of a police motor car. Sergeant Beswick stayed behind. He closed the door and gestured for Mum to go into the kitchen, then he looked up at me and my blood ran cold.

"I know this is a shock Mrs Bracken," he began. "But I have to warn you that this offence will carry a custodial sentence."

"Custodial?" I asked.

"Prison," he confirmed. He turned in my direction again. "Can I ask what you know about all this Miss Bracken?"

"Me?" I pointed to myself as if I was surprised that I was even there.

Mum wiped her face with her apron. "Kit? She has nothing to do with this."

"Is that right?" A smile crossed his face. A smile that said that he knew everything. "Mrs Bracken," he turned back to Mum, "I'm willing to give your daughter the benefit of the doubt on this occasion, but our witness didn't only see your Stan thieving from garden sheds. He also saw a girl, same age, build and height as your daughter, with her fingers on the stolen property. Now I'm sure there could be an explanation or a case of mistaken identity, so on this occasion, I'm willing to look the other way."

I will never forget the look of foul disappointment that crossed Mum's face when the policeman said those words. He turned to me. "But in return for my good favour, I expect it to stop. No more. You don't want that kind of life, trust me. Am I making myself clear?" I nodded and stepped aside as he made for the door.

"When can I see Stan?" Mum called after him.

"You can see him in court in the morning."

CHAPTER 9

"Twelve months with hard labour." The magistrate didn't listen to any arguments in Dad's favour. It turned out that he had previous for handling stolen goods when he was fourteen, so they took one look at him and saw a crook. They saw Den Bracken's son. Me and Mum and Bernie sat at the back of the courtroom and witnessed the sorry sight of Dad in the dock. He hadn't brushed his hair, he was shaking, sick from the lack of alcohol and we could see the pain in his leg was causing him bother. He looked up at us and with tears running down his face, he mouthed that he was sorry. Mum walked out of that courtroom, held onto mine and Bernie's hands and marched home with her shoulders back. She ignored the whispers from the neighbours and waited until she was sitting at the kitchen table before she crumbled. I made some tea while Bernie sat opposite her, trying to offer comfort.

"We'll be alright Mum," he said. "You never know, prison might be the best thing for Dad. It might help him with his drinking."

"How will we pay our way now?" she sobbed. "It was bad enough before, but now?"

"I'll leave school. Get a job," Bernie said. "I'm the man of the house. I'll take care of us." Mum smiled as I put the teapot on the table and joined them.

"I know you will." She wiped her cheek with the back of her hand. "But the new law says you have to stay at school until you're fourteen."

"I don't care. I'm almost fourteen," Bernie said. "I'll lie about my age."

"No. No more lying." She turned to me. "No more lying and no more stealing. Let this be a lesson to you, Kit. I don't blame you, I blame your father, but the Sergeant was right about one thing. That's not the life for you, it's not the life your father wanted for himself and it's certainly not the life he wants for you." She reached out and held our hands across the table. "We'll be alright. I don't want you to worry. We'll get through this. We'll sort something out."

It only took two months for us to fall behind and when the rent man arrived with a notice to evict, Mum had no choice. She did what she had to. She took me and Bernie to the Union Workhouse and asked them to take us in.

"It's only for a little while," she said as she handed over our bags to the matron.

"Don't worry Mrs Bracken, we'll take good care of them," the matron forced a weak smile.

"It's just until I sort things out. I need to find a place for us to stay. As soon as I do, I'll be back for them."

"Of course." The matron ushered Mum towards the door, but Mum knelt down and drew us into her.

"Look after your little sister Bernie," she said. "Look after each other. It won't be long." She kissed us both, then turning away quickly, she left us behind.

The matron's smile dropped as soon as Mum was out of the building. She rooted through our bags and told us we could have them back when we left. She led us to the bathhouse, where we were scrubbed clean in freezing water as if we had arrived covered in lice. Then we were given scratchy grey clothes to wear. Bernie left for the boy's bedroom and they threw me in with the girls. The dormitory was a bare room with brick walls and creaky floorboards. There were ten small box beds in rows on either side of the room, and each bed had at least two occupants. The smaller girls slept three or four together. As I looked around at the staring faces, a small, pale-faced girl stepped forward and took me by the hand.

"You can share with me," she said. "I'm Ned. I've had the bed to myself for a while but it's getting colder so I could do with a bedmate to keep me warm."

As she spoke, a bell rang out and all the girls lined up at the door.

"Time for tea," Ned said. "Come on. I'll show you where to go."

The matron led us down the stairs in silence to a large hall where long tables were laid out in rows. The grown up inmates sat up front and at the top there was a raised table for the governors, wardens and matrons. Some of the kitchen staff in stained white aprons walked between the tables ladling stew into the bowls in front of us. After prayers and a lecture on the rules from the head governor, we could eat. I looked around the hall for Bernie. I found him at the boy's table, with his chest out and a steely determination in his eyes.

"How long have you been here?" I asked Ned as we lay in bed that first night.

"I've always been here," she said. "I was a foundling. I never had a family."

"What never?" I couldn't imagine what that might be like, to be so alone in the world. I rolled over and looked at the dark rings under her eyes. She had a haunted expression, resigned to her life in this dark, grey building. We might not have had a home, but at least I had Bernie and Mum and Dad. At least I had a family, however broken we might be.

"It's alright," Ned smiled. "I don't mind. It's not so bad in here, you'll get used to it."

"I won't have to get used to it. Mum said she'll be back soon to fetch us."

"That's what they all say." Ned squeezed my arm and rolled over.

. . .

The workhouse was a menacing, soot blackened Victorian building with high walls that drew in around us. There were bars on all the windows, even though it wasn't a prison. A threatening atmosphere filled the air, as if violence would break out any minute. They soon put us to work to pay for our food and lodgings. We would work in the kitchen, or the laundry, or the vegetable gardens. Some boys would chop wood if they were able. I did get used to the routine of the workhouse. I suppose if you do something for long enough, you can get used to anything. The food was bland, but it was regular. The work was hard, but Ned showed me how to get by doing the least amount possible to stay out of trouble. I saw Bernie most days in the yard when they sent us out to play, whatever the weather. Someone had a football and there was always a game on. It was something familiar, something normal. A short time when we could forget where we were and just play, like we always had.

On the first Sunday of every month, the workhouse invited the board of governors and their families to dinner in the great hall. We didn't see any of it, not unless you count the potatoes that we peeled or the turnips that we chopped. We could smell it, though. A rich, mouth watering steam came off the crispy chicken skin and the aroma of goose fat on the potatoes drifted through the windows. In the gloom of a freezing December afternoon as a light snow fell, Eric Longstaff came out of the great hall with a full belly and a smirk on his face. His dad was the general manager at Carmody Cotton Mill and had been voted onto the workhouse board only a month earlier. We knew Eric from Sunday school; he was tall and handsome and good at football. He was confident in that yard, even though he was outnumbered, because he knew he was better than us. And he was right about that. He wasn't tarred with the shame of the workhouse. He could walk out of the gates and no one would stop him. Eric stood on the sidelines with his arms folded and shook his head.

"Is that the best you can do?" he laughed as Bernie scuffed his shot and the ball missed the two dustbins that did as goalposts. Bernie ignored him as he ran to fetch the ball. Eric stepped forward. "I said, is that the best you can do workhouse boy?" He looked around at all the other workhouse boys and smiled, safe in the knowledge that his higher status protected him from harm. Bernie picked up the ball and threw it to the lad in goal.

"Goal kick," he said as he returned to the middle of the yard.

"Did you hear me workhouse?" Eric said again, stepping onto the yard and taking the ball from the goalie who let him have it. "I said, is that the best you can do?" He took the football between his two hands and launched it at the back of Bernie's head. It bounced away, and I ran to collect it. Bernie's ears were glowing red. My brother was short for his age. He was stocky and had a flat crooked nose from the time I accidentally booted the ball at his face when we were small. Because of that, everyone thought he was tough. They assumed he got that nose from boxing, but he would do anything to avoid a fight. It suited him to be seen as a thug, because most of the time it kept the others from picking fights with him. It kept people at arms' length. He had to keep hold of that reputation, especially in the workhouse. It kept us safe. But it meant, at some point, he would have to prove he was up to it.

"I heard you," Bernie said slowly.

"So what's your answer?" Eric folded his arms and leaned back.

"Even on my worst day, I'm better than you. I can tell that from looking at your lanky legs."

Bernie looked him up and down and everyone in the yard laughed. Bernie nodded at me to throw him the ball.

"Are you looking for a fight?" Eric said, not wanting to lose face.

"I'm not going to fight you," Bernie said, bouncing the ball under his foot and putting his hands on his hips, waiting for Eric to move on so we could restart the game. Bernie knew that even if he won in a fight against Eric, he would still be the loser. Fighting with the son of a director would not end well for Bernie.

"So you're a coward. Just like your waste of space of a father. No wonder you ended up in a place like this."

"Fine. Let's do it." Bernie kicked the ball away and rolled up his sleeves. He was calling Eric's bluff, hoping that he would refuse a fist fight. But before Eric could do anything, there was a sudden, loud rap on the window. One of the wardens was watching on. He gestured for everyone to move away.

Eric smiled. "What's the problem? Scared of the wardens? I thought as much. Scrapping is the one thing you're good at, and you can't even do that."

"This isn't over," Bernie said.

"Oh, I think it is."

"I can't beat you here, not with the wardens looking on, but I'll beat you outside. You and me, bare knuckle. A proper fight." It was a hollow threat. Eric was no more up for a real fight than Bernie was.

"No, let's settle this like honourable men," Eric said, looking round for approval. "Not something you Brackens know much about, honour, but it'll make a change for you."

"Do you want to take me on or not?"

"Penalties." Eric folded his arms. "This started with football. We should settle it with football."

"Fine." Bernie picked up the ball.

"No, not now." Eric looked back at the window. "Next week, at the Sidings. A proper goal with a proper net. Best of five. That is, if you're allowed out." He held out his hand. "What do you say?"

Bernie looked around at the excited faces. "Best of five." He shook Eric's hand, and the game was on.

CHAPTER 10

By Saturday afternoon, the snow was thick on the ground. It didn't put anyone off. Bernie and Eric's penalty shootout was the talk of the town. Some lads in the workhouse stayed behind to cover for us, and a small delegation, including me and Ned, followed Bernie out of the gap in the fence and over to the football field. The Sidings was packed. A group of volunteers had shovelled the snow from in front of the goalmouth. Bernie was nervous. I could see it, but no one else could.

"Just take your time," I told him as we walked through the crowd and onto the pitch. "You can shoot penalties in your sleep."

"I know Kit," he said.

"Pick your spot and don't change your mind."

"Kit, please. I know how to take a penalty," he smiled, and I knew he would be alright.

Eric was waiting for us. A referee was chosen, a terrified boy who took his role seriously. They would take each penalty against a goalkeeper of Eric and Bernie's choosing. They would play the best of five. If they were equal after five shots, they would go on in a sudden death shoot out. The first to miss would lose.

Eric won the coin toss and went first. The crowd was silent until the ball hit the back of the net, then a cheer went up from his supporters.

Bernie was next. He placed the ball on the spot, took a few steps back and drove the ball through the keeper. One a piece. They both scored the next, then the third. Eric stepped up for the fourth.

A shout came from the crowd. "Take your time, posh boy!" it was Charlie Ross, one of Bernie's friends from school. He was quickly shushed, but it had the desired effect. Eric scuffed his shot, and the keeper batted it away. Bernie stepped forward. It all came down to this.

"Come on, Bernie lad," someone called from the crowd.

"Get back to scrubbing floors, workhouse boy,"

another voice said. Bernie looked over. I shook my head, telling him to ignore it. But it was too late. Bernie's mind wasn't on the task at hand. I saw his eyes pick his spot. The top right corner. But then he changed his mind. He should never have changed his mind. Pick your spot and stick to it. The goalie moved first. Bernie saw an opening and went for it. But the indecision affected his kick, and there was no power to it. The goalkeeper's trailing leg knocked the ball away. There was a groan from the crowd. It was exhausting watching in the freezing cold and everyone wanted it to be over. But it was far from done. Both Eric and Bernie refocused and scored the next attempt. It was down to sudden death. But they matched each other, shot for shot. The duel went on. Fifteen, twenty, twenty-five a piece. If Eric scored, Bernie scored. If Eric missed, Bernie missed. Neither of them would give up. The light faded and some of the crowd drifted away.

"This can't go on much longer," the referee said, looking at his watch. The goalkeepers were exhausted. It was as much a duel for them as it was for Eric and Bernie. "We have to settle it."

"I'm not losing this on the toss of a coin," Bernie said, resting his hands on his knees.

"Me neither," Eric agreed. "How about we nominate someone to take the shot for us?"

They scanned the crowd. There was a flurry of unease. Most people wishing they had gone home when they had the chance. No one wanted the honour of being chosen, only to fail in the attempt. It would never be forgotten.

"Let's keep it in the family," Bernie looked up. "My sister against yours. Kit Bracken versus Aggie Longstaff."

Eric laughed. "Are you serious?"

"Why not? We have to settle it somehow. What better way than your sister against mine?"

My cheeks burned as everyone looked in my direction. Bernie turned to me and nodded. I wanted the ground to swallow me up, but something in Bernie's eyes told me to trust him, so I puffed out my chest and stood firm. Looking down the line, I made eye contact with Aggie Longstaff. I didn't know Aggie. She was older than me, but not by much. Where I was short and scruffy, she was tall and smart. She dressed well and carried herself with a confidence that I could never hold. She wasn't a workhouse girl after all, not like me. Bernie took me by the arm.

"Are you ready for this?" he asked.

"I… I don't know."

"You can do it. You've done it a hundred times before. How many times do you think Aggie Longstaff has kicked a ball?" I looked over at her. She was fuming with Eric, she pushed him away and made for the exit. But Eric pulled her back and calmed her. Bernie had a point. I understood why he had made the suggestion. We Brackens might not have much going for us, but we know how to kick a football.

Aggie and I stepped forward in front of the crowd. Anyone who was planning on leaving stayed to witness the action. We flipped a coin. Aggie called heads and won. She would go first. Bernie and I stood back to watch. Eric took her to one side, giving her some last-minute coaching tips, but she shrugged him off. Then it was Aggie on her own versus the goalkeeper. She hitched up her skirt to free her legs. The goalkeeper smiled and jumped up and down on the spot. He was confident he could save a shot against a girl. Aggie turned without stopping to compose herself or pick a spot. She ran at the ball and kicked it with all her strength. The goalkeeper was caught off guard; he lunged at the ball too late as it passed by at head height and swished into the back of the net. There was silence as the crowd adjusted their expectation to the reality of what they had seen. It wasn't over yet. If I could score, the contest would go on.

"Right, you can do this Kit," Bernie said, handing me the ball. "If she can do it, you can do it."

I nodded and stepped onto the penalty spot. All eyes were on me. It was as if my every move was magnified. I struggled to put one foot in front of the other. I could hear the voices from the sidelines.

"This'll be funny, there's nothing of her," someone said.

"Bernie is an idiot. Why did he suggest this? There's no way she can score."

Bernie steered me away. "Ignore them. Focus on the ball. No one else is here. It's just you, the ball and back of the net. Score the goal. You can do this, Kit Bracken."

He stepped away, and I placed the ball on the ground. I looked up at the goalposts. My hands were cold and clammy. My heart was thumping in my throat and pounding in my ears. I took three steps back and closed my eyes. Just me, the ball and the back of the net. My run up was short, but I got my foot right underneath the ball. I used my entire body to get power in my shot, so much so that I lost balance and fell over. There was silence as I watched the ball fly up, up, and up. It was going all the way, but it was off target. It smacked against the wooden goalpost and bounced back towards me. There was a cheer from Eric and his pals. Everyone was laughing. My knees stung from the hard, frosty ground. I looked at Bernie. His head dropped but he hauled me to my feet.

"It wasn't my fault," I said under my breath. "Someone put me off. Did you hear it? Someone in the crowd."

Bernie walked away as Eric came over with his hand outstretched. Bernie took a firm hold.

"Never mind workhouse boy," Eric laughed, looking back at his pals.

"You better stay away from me, Longstaff," Bernie said. "You don't know what 'workhouse' boys are capable of!"

CHAPTER 11

Mum came for us as she promised she would. She had a plan. Now Bernie was old enough, he would have to leave school and start at the hatworks. The new end terrace she had found needed both their wages. We couldn't rely on Dad anymore. When he came out of prison, he was a shadow of the man he once was. He had aged ten years, was skinny and unsteady on his feet and blamed himself for our decline into the workhouse. He gave in to a life in a drunken haze. Almost as soon as Bernie began his new job, he joined the football team. The hatworks run of success in the Viaduct cup had ended with Dad's injury and in the years since they hadn't got as far as the quarterfinals. Bernie changed all that.

He had the Bracken's natural talent and a burning desire to finish what Dad had started.

"You should work on passing across the field," I shouted from the sidelines as the hatworks team trained in the park. "Let me show you." I ran on and collected the ball. "See Alf won't be marked all the way over there." The boys stopped playing and Charlie Ross, the goalkeeper, came and took the ball from me.

"This is a proper training session, Kit. You can't keep interfering."

"I'm not interfering," I said, trying to take the ball back. "You could get past their defence if you send in some long crosses."

"Bernie? Will you tell her? This isn't a kick about in the schoolyard, it's the real thing."

Bernie ran over and I snatched the ball back, expecting my brother to tell Charlie to listen to my advice, but he didn't stand up for me.

"You should go home Kit," Bernie said.

"Go home?"

"Charlie's right. We're not children anymore. This is a man's game now. We need your support, but not on the pitch." He took the ball from me.

"But I can help."

"From the sidelines," he gestured for me to leave

the field. I was so shocked that I did as he asked. Until that point, football had always been our thing, mine and Bernie's and Dad's. Now it was being taken away from me. I had always played football, always dribbled a ball around town, always spent my free time in the park or at the Sidings or simply kicking the ball against the wall in the ginnel at the side of our house. For the first time, it dawned on me that as I grew older I might not be able to play. Men played all their lives if they wanted, they played with their pals, then with their sons, but you never saw women playing, not grown women. It horrified me. The thought of the one thing I loved more than anything being taken away. But I did as Bernie asked, and I supported them from the sidelines. I was there when they lost sixteen nil to a team of railway workers. I was there when they won on penalties against the colliers from Hexelby Mine. I saved my comments and suggestions for when I was alone with Bernie and he passed them on to the team. I was there at every game, home and away, rain or shine, win or lose. So when they eventually made it to the final of the Viaduct Cup in 1913, it was as if I were about to line up next to them on the pitch.

CHAPTER 12

"Quiet please ladies and gentlemen," the fairground man in the bowler hat quietened the crowd as Dad nodded to Len Murgotroyd in goal. A hush fell over the street, even the silver band stopped playing. Only the chatter of the organ grinder's monkey broke the silence. Dad turned and hopped towards the ball. He missed. I don't mean he missed the penalty; I mean, he missed the ball. His leg swung wildly, and he ended up in a heap on the ground. The crowd erupted into snorts of laughter. Dad scrambled to his feet, rubbing his bad leg. "Again," he said. "One more go. I've got my eye in now." I didn't stay to watch. I've seen my father make a fool of himself plenty of times. For Dad, it is always what could have been. If it hadn't been for that injury, he could have been a hero. He could have lifted the cup.

I joined Mum on the wooden terrace to watch Bernie's match. We cheered as the team ran out from the changing room under the first arch of the bridge. Bernie looked up and smiled as he lined up in his smart green kit and polished boots. I saw Dad in the crowd opposite, drowning his shame from a bottle in a brown paper bag. It was a frantic match right from the starting whistle. The teams fought a battle on the pitch, but neither could break through the defences. They went into the break goalless, but the Hatters had a share of the shots on goal, so the momentum was on their side. It would all come down to who could hold their nerve. We had planned for this, me and Bernie. A week before the game, we sat on the grass watching the lads in training.

"Do you believe we can do it?" Bernie asked me. "Do you think we could really beat Carmody Mill and win the cup?"

"Of course I do," I answered smartly. "And so should you. Believe it otherwise it won't happen." He was always like this before a big game, nervous, doubting his abilities. Probably because it meant so much. His confidence would drain away and he'd turn into the frightened workhouse boy putting on a front.

"They're good, though, Carmody Mill," Bernie said.

"They're good, but they're not unbeatable. You can match them man for man."

"Matching them won't be enough. We need something extra, something special."

"That's you, Bernie. You're the something special. You're the best player we've ever had."

"I'm not sure about that," he pulled his cap down to hide his blushes. "I wish we could get you on the pitch," he nudged me.

"Don't be daft. Girls don't play football. Not properly."

"But that would give them something to think about, wouldn't it? With your skills, you could weave between them, leave them on your heels. They wouldn't get near you."

"It's you they should be worried about," I said. "They don't know what workhouse boys are capable of."

. . .

The Bamford Hatters came out after the break with their heads all over the place. Their defence crumbled as Carmody Mill slotted in two goals in quick succession. But the Bamford boys were used to fighting back and scrambled an opening goal over the line. With the wind at their backs, they pushed forward and took advantage of a sloppy defensive pass and equalised. With ten minutes left to play, a frustrated wayward tackle resulted in a free kick to the Hatters just outside the Carmody penalty box. Bernie set the ball down. He looked up to find me in the stands and I nodded. He picked his spot, and I knew he couldn't miss. Bernie drew his foot back and struck the ball with power and accuracy. It sailed over the heads of the defenders, who jumped in unison. The keeper leapt for the top corner of his goal, but he was too slow. The ball skimmed the inside edge of the goalpost and went into the net. He'd done it. The momentary silence of the crowd was replaced by a cheer the likes of which the Sidings football ground had never heard. Bamford Hatworks were a goal ahead, with minutes to play.

Despite their lead, the Hatters weren't content. They only had to defend, but they pushed on. Charlie Ross left his goalmouth and struck for goal from the halfway line. He hit it well, but the ball ricocheted off the Carmody defenders in the penalty box and hit the post. There was a grumble from the crowd. Eric Longstaff, now the captain of the Carmody team, lunged to clear the ball off the line. As his foot followed through, his boot struck Bernie full in the face. Eric raised his hands in apology and turned away. Bernie wiped the blood from his mouth with his sleeve. The Carmody players had been going after Bernie all match; late tackles, elbows in his ribs, pulling at his shirt and Bernie had kept his cool, but this was the final straw. In a moment of retaliation, he pushed Eric from behind and watched as he stumbled and fell.

The referee blew his whistle and pointed at Bernie. Before he knew it, several Carmody players barrelled into Bernie, pushing him in defence of their captain. The Bamford boys joined in, arms flailing, football forgotten as a brawl broke out. The crowd went wild. Some spectators even ran on to join in. It took a good ten minutes for the referee to calm everything and the police had to blow their whistles to chase away the spectators. We watched in horror as the referee called Bernie over, took out his book, and sent him off. The crowd booed as he walked away with his shoulders slumped. I will never know if those boos were for Bernie or the referee's decision, but I do know the only thing Bernie heard were the jeers aimed at him. The last ten minutes passed in a blur. The Bamford boys were lost without their captain. Carmody took advantage against ten men and scored two rapid goals against an exhausted defence. The game ended four- three to Carmody Mill.

Mum made us stay to watch them lift the trophy, even though all I wanted to do was run away.

"It's not fair," I said. "Bernie did nothing wrong. They cheated. It's not fair."

"Whoever said the world was fair, Kit? We should lose with honour." She gripped my arm. It was a stupid thing to say. They robbed us, they didn't win with honour, so why should we applaud them? I caught sight of Bernie, changed back into his everyday clothes, his collar up and his cap pulled low. He was leaning against the wall, his arms folded. As Eric Longstaff raised the Viaduct Cup and the crowd roared, he turned and walked away.

CHAPTER 13

We sat at the kitchen table in silence. Mum stirred a pan of fried liver and onions. Bernie's head was down, a black eye, split lip and scratches on his neck were proof of the battle he had fought on the pitch. We were so close. So very close.

"You did your best. That's all anyone can ask of you," Mum said finally. Bernie clenched his fists. Mum placed a plate in front of him and put her hand on his. "No more fighting."

"They did it on purpose," he said. "Eric Longstaff with his freckles and smarmy grin. He's got it coming to him."

"No, he hasn't." Mum passed a plate for me.

"No more. And that goes for you too, Kit." She pointed the wooden spoon at me.

"What did I do?" I asked, wide eyed.

Mum filled her own plate and slammed the pan back onto the stovetop. "We are better than that," she said, sitting down. She was wrong. We weren't better than that. 'That' is exactly what we were, and the entire town knew it. A family of thieves, drunks and backstreet brawlers. We stiffened as we heard the children playing in the street scatter, then the click of the back gate and the scrape of the privy door. We listened to the sound of Dad emptying his bladder of the ale he had spent the afternoon drinking. He stumbled against the metal dustbin before falling in through the kitchen door.

"Where is he?" he said through gritted teeth.

Bernie backed away while Mum stepped forward to stand between them.

"No, Stan," she said. "Leave him be."

"Leave him be? Leave him be? After that shower of a performance."

"He did his best, Stan," Mum gestured for Bernie to leave.

Dad had only just started. "You made a show of me today, lad!" there was a string of spittle hanging from his mouth, "in front of the entire town. We had a chance, but you blew it!" Dad was shouting now.

Mum tried to push him away, but he lost his balance and his flailing arm knocked her square in the face. She fell backwards against the stove. That was enough for Bernie. He faced up to Dad, pushed him against the wall and raised his fist. Dad didn't put up a fight, not physically. He was too drunk for that. But he wasn't done fighting with his words.

"Go on then. Hit me. No, of course you won't. You haven't got the bottle. You've no backbone, no brains. Hit me. Do something for once. That was the best chance we ever had to win the cup and you blew it."

Mum tried to stand but couldn't get her balance. "Bernie don't. Please don't," she said with her hand over her mouth.

Bernie tightened his grip. "You always said you wanted me to be a better man than you. Well, that's not hard. I am twice the man you will ever be," he lowered his fist and let go, pushing Dad out of the kitchen into the yard. Dad slurred his words as he clambered to his feet.

"That's right. It's all my fault. You lose the cup and it's all my fault. Never could do anything right by you, could I?"

CHAPTER 14

Mum had to persuade Bernie to go back into work on the Monday after the match.

"You have to face up to it sometime. These things happen. Hold your head up," she said as she poured the tea at breakfast.

"Hold my head up?" he bowed his head low, as if to make his point. "They sent me off. How can I hold my head up?"

"No one blames you," I said to him. But that wasn't true. Everyone blamed Bernie. I'd heard a man in the crowd telling his wife as much; "If only he'd kept his head. We had it. We were touching the trophy, and then a Bracken came along to ruin it."

I didn't tell Bernie that. "The team wouldn't

have even been in the cup final if it wasn't for you," I insisted.

We walked into work together. Some of the lads from the team were huddled in a group in the yard.

"Decided to show your face, have you?" Charlie Ross called over.

"Ignore them." I held on to Bernie's arm.

"No, Mum's right. I need to face up to it." He removed my hand and went over to them. "Lads, what can I say? It wasn't my fault, that lad Eric kicked me in the face."

"Then you pushed him." Ronnie Squire wasn't in a forgiving mood. "You gifted them the trophy."

"He threw himself on the floor. You saw what happened. I barely touched him."

"I could accept it if they had been the better team, but we had them on the ropes. We were in the lead. All we had to do was run down the clock but you had to try and settle old scores."

"I'm sorry," Bernie said. "I shouldn't have pushed him, but he…."

"Always with the excuses. You sound just like your old dad. Sorry isn't good enough," Beckett said. "Here, this is yours, not that you deserve it." He fished a medal out of his pocket and threw it over, the ribbon created a flight in the air as it sailed towards Bernie's hand.

"What is it?" I asked, as he caught it.

"It's the loser's medal," he stuffed it into his pocket as the lads from the team went inside.

"They'll come round. It was an accident. They're just disappointed that's all," I said.

The whistle went for the start of the shift. Mr Grimes, the foreman, stood at the door. "Come on now. Inside. Let's start the day. A word Bernie," he called Bernie over. "I don't want any trouble, lad. There's a lot of angry people in this factory after that performance of yours on Saturday."

"I'm sorry, sir," Bernie said, his humiliation complete.

"Don't say sorry to me. I never believed we could win the cup, so it's no skin off my nose. But I don't want any trouble. If anyone fronts up to you, walk away. Do you understand? I won't have any scrapping over this."

"No sir."

"On your way then."

Bernie went off to the packing room with his head down and his hands in his pockets.

"Mr Grimes?" I followed him in. "Mr Grimes, can I ask about my application?"

"Your application?" He took out his pocket watch and herded the latecomers to their work stations.

"To move into the trimming room?" I started work at Bamford's on my fourteenth birthday. All the girls start in cutting, we measure out and cut the cloth to make the hats. But the best job of all is in trimming, where the hats are finished off and you can really see the result of your work.

"Ah yes," he turned. "I'm afraid that there are no vacancies in trimming at the moment."

"But when there are, can I get the position?"

"We'll have to see about that. There may be better candidates."

"But I asked first, sir. Shouldn't I be the first choice?"

"Progression isn't guaranteed just because you ask for it."

"Why not? Haven't I earned it?"

He laughed. "Earned it? Miss Bracken, perhaps if you showed some diligence you might have already moved up by now."

"Diligence?"

"Hard work, Miss Bracken. Perhaps if you were on time more often, if your productivity was better and the standard of your work was up to scratch, maybe then you might have achieved promotion. I suggest you spend more time concentrating on the task in hand instead of daydreaming about football. Perhaps then, you might progress. Think on Miss Bracken. Think on." He tapped his watch and gestured towards the cutting room.

CHAPTER 15

D ad stayed away for three days and then crawled back, full of remorse and apologies.

"I've signed the pledge," he said. "No more drinking."

"You've signed the temperance pledge before," Mum said, the yellow bruise on her face fading.

"This time it's different. This time I'll stick to it."

He didn't, of course. After a calm few weeks, he came home late with the smell of ale on his breath. It wasn't long before he stayed out all night, and we knew he had fallen back into his old ways.

Bernie was taunted and ridiculed everywhere he went. There was even talk of him being dropped from the team. If he hadn't been such a skilful player, he would have been out long since.

After weeks of Bernie's moping, Mum had seen enough. She threw open his curtains and wouldn't let him sleep in.

"What's wrong with you?" she said.

"What do you think?"

"I think you need to stop feeling sorry for yourself and get back out there."

"What's the point?" He pulled his pillow over his face to block out the light. "I'm going back to sleep."

"No, you're not. It's Sunday, don't you have football training?"

"They don't want me on the team anymore. You were there, you saw what happened."

"And you're happy to leave it at that, are you?"

"What choice do I have?" Bernie sat up.

"You made it to the final of the Viaduct Cup. I don't know how you can see that as a failure."

"We didn't win. Of course it was a failure."

Mum put her hand into her apron pocket and pulled out the runners up medal.

"Where did you get that?" Bernie asked.

"I fished it out of the bin where you threw it."

"That's where it belongs."

"They don't give these out to just anyone you know. You might think this medal means failure, but this means the world to me. To me, this tells of all the hours you dedicated to training, in the mud and the snow and the rain. It tells of all the matches you played to get to the final. This medal tells me everything I need to know about my son Bernie Bracken, and I couldn't be prouder," she threw it on to the bed. "What matters now is what you do next. You need to show courage. The wonderful thing about the Viaduct Cup is they play it every year. If you miss out one year, you can try again the next."

It was a revelation. He could try again. If he won the cup in 1914, the shame of the defeat would wash away. He could wipe 1913 from the history books. He went to training that afternoon. I watched from the sidelines as he stood back. In the end, the ball came to him and they waved him on. Six long months later, a season of hard fought games, and they secured their place in the final. Carmody Mill qualified too, of course. It would be a rematch. Except this time, the outcome would be different.

CHAPTER 16

"One more game," Bernie said as we sat by the lake in the park. The silver band was playing in the bandstand and children laughed as they fed the ducks. It was a sunny bank holiday Monday, the day of the annual Bamford Hatworks family picnic, and everything was right with the world.

"One more game and we've done it. We need to keep calm," Bernie was coaching himself. He had learnt his lesson. "How do you think they're doing?" he asked, pulling at a handful of grass.

"You need to remind Ronnie to not run ahead of the ball," I said. "He keeps doing it. They'll tackle him too easily. You should play Beckett on the right wing. That Carmody Mill outside left is fast, but he's weak. Beckett can muscle him out of the game." I lay back on my elbows.

"Who do you think should take the penalties?" Bernie asked.

"That's tricky. You, of course. But their goalie will have done his research on you. You should have someone else ready."

"What about Alf Kershaw? It's likely to be his last match. He'll want to go out on a victory."

"You want to pick someone for old time's sake?" I laughed.

"No, but it would be nice after all the years he's given to the team."

"Nice? Bernie this is the final of the Viaduct Cup! There's no room for nice."

"I'm not being nice. I'm Bernie Bracken, remember. Tough nut. I'm not nice." He nudged me and laughed.

Everything was falling in to place. But the world, it seemed, had an alternative plan.

As we sat in the sunshine, with our familiar world of smoky chimneys and football all around us, something shifted. A shout from the market-place, a ripple of something invisible rustled through the trees. The silver band stopped play-ing, the church bells rang out. Then Terry

Mossop ran towards us, waving a copy of the Chronicle.

"War!" he said. "We're going to war!"

The country was at war. But we took no notice. We had a more important battle on our hands. The night before the match, we walked down to the pitch at the Sidings for a kick about. I wanted to make sure nothing would upset Bernie. But what we found upset us both. The army had moved in. Tents and horses covered the pitch and soldiers were running their bayonets at sand bags. Bernie dropped the football and ran to the middle.

"What is this? What's happening here?" he said to the nearest officer, who was marking a list on a clipboard.

"What does it look like?" he said, paying no attention.

"You're ruining the pitch," Bernie said desperately. "Did no one tell you there's a cup final here tomorrow?"

"Did nobody tell you there's a war on, son?" he quipped back, smirking.

"You can't be here. You have to leave, come back next week. Look at the damage you're doing to the grass!" Bernie picked up a crate as if he could single-handedly move the entire army camp off the pitch.

"Put that down lad," the soldier turned serious. "This land has been commandeered by his majesty's government. It is an offence to obstruct an officer in the execution of his duties. I'll tell you one more time, son. Put that down and clear off."

I saw the commotion from the window of the cutting room. It was the middle of the morning, so all the workers should have been at their posts, but a group of lads had gathered in the yard.

"Your work is in front of you Miss Bracken, not out of the window." the supervisor, Mrs Miller looked up from her desk and gestured for me to return to my work. I flattened the cloth in front of me and began the measurements, but I could hear raised voices outside. I looked down the line at the girls with their measuring sticks and chalk marking out the pattern and turned back to the thick black cloth in front of me. Picking up my shears I looked out of the window again and saw Bernie with his hands in his pockets joining the ever-growing group of young men.

"Excuse me, Mrs Miller. Can I go to the toilet?" I asked, shuffling on my feet to make it seem like I was desperate.

"You can go at break time," she answered without looking up.

"It's urgent!" I said, edging towards the door.

Mrs Miller sighed. "Very well. Straight there and back, if you're over five minutes, you can stay behind at dinner. Next time, go before the shift…"

I didn't wait around to hear the rest of her speech; I darted for the door. There was an excitement in the air as if something had changed, but the big machines were still thumping, banging the hats into shape. As I passed the blocking room the carpenters were hammering away at their chisels, making the wooden moulds. The women in trimming were singing as they concentrated on the finishing touches. I followed Walter Winstanley as he came out of the blocking room and joined the others in the yard. Bernie's cheeks were flushed as he stood in the centre of the group.

"But what about the football?" he said. "We'll have to wait for them to reschedule the final."

"They'll need to wait until we've won the war," Charlie Ross said to the agreement of the others.

"We?" I asked as I pushed my way to the centre.

"Well, not you girls. Of course not. Us lads. They're asking for men to join up."

"Men?" I scoffed.

"Yes, men. We're all going to the town hall. They've got up a recruitment office. They've said we can all go together. All us pals fighting the war together. In France. Finally, we can get out of 'Never' Bridge and see the world. You're coming with us, aren't you Bernie?"

"After the match, though. After we've played the final?"

"Forget the football," Charlie said. "We're off to war!"

CHAPTER 17

Bernie came home for two days leave before he was shipped off to France. Little Andrew from next door led a line of small children who paraded after him down the street. Andrew marched with a broom handle over his shoulder and Bernie let him wear his cap. Mum cried when she saw Bernie in his uniform. I don't know if she was proud or scared. But he looked smart and important. Mum had imagined her children toiling at the hatworks for the rest of our lives. Now here was Bernie in the uniform of the King's army. He stood to attention in the kitchen while mum stepped back to examine him. She wiped away her tears and pulled out her tin of hidden money from under the stove.

"Here." She counted out the hot coins and handed them to Bernie. "Run to the photographic shop in town and get a portrait done." She looked at me and counted out some more. "Kit, get washed and changed into your Sunday best. I want both of you in a photograph. We should remember a day like this."

We weren't the only family wanting a portrait done before the boys left for the front. We waited in the queue on the street.

Bernie cleared his throat. "Kit," he said my name sincerely, so I knew he was about to be serious. "When I'm away, you will take care of Mum, won't you?"

"Of course I will." He didn't have to ask.

"I mean with Dad. I won't be there to stand between them and I'm worried that.."

"Bernie, I can handle Dad. You know that."

"But if I don't come back, then I…"

"Why wouldn't you come back? You've got a cup final to win."

On the way home, we bumped into Dad in the market square. He didn't realise it was us at first. He had been out drinking and was asking passers-by for small change.

"Oh, it's you, is it?" Dad said when he looked back. "Come to show off in your fancy uniform?"

"Nothing changes, does it Dad, eh?" Bernie said. "Look at the state of you."

"You mind your own business," Dad said. He was incapable of finding any decent words.

"It is my business if you go home and cause bother for Mum and our Kit."

"Bother?" he slurred. "I'm no bother to them. Am I Kit?" He looked at me for backup.

"He's alright Bernie, leave him." I pulled him away.

"Here." Bernie took some coins from his pocket. "Take this."

"I don't need your charity," Dad said.

"Fair enough," Bernie said. "Call it rent."

Dad grunted, then took the money.

"Just to see me right," Dad insisted. "Then I'll sign the pledge. You'll see."

"Course you will, Dad," Bernie said sadly. "See you around then." We walked away. There were tears in Bernie's eyes, but he didn't blink them free.

"Bernie?" Dad called after us. We turned. "You

look after yourself, lad. Out there. You take care son."

CHAPTER 18

Dear Kit,

I was very glad indeed to receive your letter. I hope you are keeping out of trouble. Well, we are now in France. We marched for days on end and my feet are torn to shreds, but we have made camp and we can rest now. We are very close to the 5th battalion. We are all a part of the same regiment, so it's not too much of a surprise. But you will never guess who is with them? Eric Longstaff. He came over to shake my hand and hope for no hard feelings. Let me tell you Kit, a year ago I would have knocked his teeth out. But it seemed wrong to fight him, when we are on the same side. So I shook his hand and said I was glad to know him. But if I'm ever on a football pitch with him again, I won't hold back. Well, I'd better leave off and get some sleep. We never know when we may be called upon to keep moving.

Ta ta for now,

Your brother

Bernie.

Dear Bernie,

I hope you are keeping well. There isn't much doing, here at home. Mum has got a different job at the hatworks looking after the new girls who have replaced all you lads. Dad is doing alright. He has picked up some more work on the rag and bone round so you need not worry on that front. Mr Bamford has brought in a new contract and we will now make the caps and helmets for officers as well as enlisted men. I have applied to move into the trimming room or to be a supervisor in cutting, but I don't think old man Grimes is keen.

Carmody Mill have switched off their cotton looms and converted to making munitions. There are handbills around town encouraging people to work there. The money is good, they say, but the work is hard and dangerous. They have to fill shell casings with explosives. I would never work for

Carmody Mill. Even if they paid me double. We're hatters and that's that. And what we do is working towards the war effort too. We miss you terribly and hope you will come home soon. I have included a parcel with fruit cake and cigarettes.

Write again soon,

Your loving sister

Kit

Dear Kit,

I'm sure you will have heard about Charlie Ross by now. It was a terrible day, but I don't believe he knew much about it, which should be a comfort. He was my friend and I will miss him. It makes me want to fight harder, to win the war for him and for all the others. Me and the boys had a drink for him last night in a local estaminet. That's like a French pub, with red wine and warm ale. Please let me know any news from home, I find myself thinking fondly of old Nether Bridge.

Well, I am tired and must rise early to move on. Remember me to Mrs Ross and tell her I am thinking of her family at this sad time.

Ta ta for now,

Your brother,

Bernie

Dear Bernie,

I cannot tell you the shock at the news of Charlie Ross. His mother bore the burden well and even came into work. She said she has to keep busy and do as much as she can for the war effort, and to support her other five sons at the front. It is a very sad time and we worry greatly for you. Please do not take any risks. News from home...A tram car derailed last week. No one was injured, but there were delays all afternoon. The price of bread has gone up again. Mum has written to Mr Lloyd George himself to protest at the price increase. As soon as she posted the letter, the newspaper reported that he is supporting a bill to close the pubs early and stop people from drinking too much. A cause she supports, of course. So she immediately wrote again to apologise about her earlier letter. If she gets a reply, I will let you know.

Well, that's all for now.

I remain your loving sister,

Kit

. . .

Dear Kit,

I hope you are keeping well, as I am. Please forgive my handwriting. I am sitting in the corner of a trench in the dead of night and it is so cold I can barely grip the pencil. So much for summer being warmer. I dread to think what the winter will be like. Let's hope it's all over by then. We have all had enough now, and although we try to keep our spirits high, I do long for home.

I trust that work is going well at the hatworks. I often look at the seams of my hat and wonder if it was finished in the trimming room at Bamfords and you or Mum or one of the others had a hand in the stitching. It's seen me through a few sticky moments has this hat, well I'm still here, so it must be my lucky charm.

We had some new lads arrive earlier this week. Kit, they look so young. Is that what we were like when we arrived? So young and fresh faced and eager to please? I can't imagine it. I saw a private soldier last week who must have been fifty-five if he was a day, round as a jelly baby he was. Are they taking young boys and older men now? What will happen when all the men are gone? Will they send the women and then the children until there is no one left? Come to think of it, I'm sure you girls would make a better fist of it than we have.

I shall leave off for now as the light is fading and I am due on sentry duty. Ronnie sends his fond regards and says if I don't take his place at the parapet, he will write to you himself. And you don't want to hear whatever he has to say.

Ta ta for now,

Your loving brother,

Bernie.

CHAPTER 19

Bernie came home on leave in May 1916. I was so excited, I snuck out of work early so I could meet him at the railway station. It was worth the telling off I knew I would get from the new supervisor. Bernie only had a week of leave, which meant that after the travelling, he would have three days with us. It wasn't long enough at all, so I wanted to make the most of it.

"Bernie!" I spotted him straight away as he stepped off the train, even though there were loads of other soldiers in the same uniform.

"Kit," he smiled. "Shouldn't you be at work?"

"I couldn't miss meeting you off the train." I had his old football with me. "Maybe we could have a kick about before we go home? Like the old times?" I said when he looked at the ball tucked under my arm.

"Maybe later. I just want to get home."

It was disappointing, but he'd had a long, exhausting journey. "I'll draw you a bath when we get in. It's not Sunday, but I'm sure we can make an exception."

"It's in everyone's best interests if I have a bath. These clothes need washing as well. They stink." He did smell; of smoke and damp and sweat and mud. The hem of his coat was thick with it. "How is everyone?" he asked. He didn't mean everyone, he meant Dad. Was Dad drinking? What would he find when he got home?

"Alright. Mum works a lot now. We've got ever such a lot of work on."

"And Dad?"

"Oh, you know Dad. We haven't seen him for a while." That wasn't always a good sign. The calm of him not being around normally meant he was out somewhere drinking and when he finally came home, it was for money or for a fight.

"And he's been alright with Mum?"

"For the most part."

"I try to ask in my letters, but she doesn't give much away."

"She doesn't want you to worry."

"Do I have anything to worry about?" He stopped.

"No," I said it convincingly, because it was true. Dad hadn't changed, but we could handle him.

It took a while to get home, because everyone stopped us to shake Bernie's hand and ask about the front, ask if he had seen their son or brother out there. Bernie was polite, but he didn't say much. He could answer all the questions without giving any real information. He said things like, 'oh you know how it is.' And 'we're all getting stuck in' and 'they don't know what's hit them.'

After a bath and a hot meal, he fell asleep in front of the fire in the kitchen. Me and Mum couldn't stop looking at him. He was our Bernie alright, but he was different. It was as if he was home, but he wasn't fully home, like he had left something behind. Mum patted his leg.

"Why don't you go up to bed," she said. "I'll bring you a cup of tea."

Bernie slept for the rest of the afternoon, all night and most of the following morning. I was impatient for him to wake up. He didn't have enough time as it was, and he was going to waste most of it sleeping?

"We should wake him up," I said. "He won't sleep tonight."

"Leave him be." Mum had noticed a change in Bernie too. Maybe she thought he would sleep it off and the Bernie who woke would be back to normal. "He must need the sleep. It's a terrible strain on them out there at the front."

When he did finally wake, he seemed more exhausted than ever. He ate quietly, staring into the fire.

"Fancy a kick about?" I asked, bouncing the ball.

"Not in the house," Mum said.

"Let's go to the Sidings. The goalposts are still up." I threw the ball to Bernie, who caught it and reluctantly followed me out. We didn't make it to the field. As we passed the Spinner's Arms, an old friend of Bernie's stopped him in the street.

"Will you let me buy you a pint, lad?" he said. "You boys are doing such a wonderful job, it's the least I can do."

Bernie looked at me and I nodded. "We can play later on," I said. I went to the football field on my own and ran about, kicking the ball against the wall. I was lonelier than ever, even though Bernie was home. There was no 'later on' that day. Bernie didn't come back from the pub until dark. I heard him stagger in through the backyard as I lay in bed. It was a familiar sound, but it was heartbreaking to look out of my window to see that it was Bernie, drunk out of his mind and not Dad. The next day, I didn't ask him to come and play football with me. It didn't seem like he wanted to. So when he finished his breakfast and picked up the ball, I abandoned my porridge. "Shall we?" he smiled.

"After church," Mum said.

"Church?" Bernie and I said in unison. "Since when do we go to church?" I asked.

"It's not Christmas, is it?" Bernie laughed.

"No," Mum dusted down her best coat. "But it may as well be. We have you home, safe with us, and we ought to give thanks."

There was no arguing with that.

Church with Bernie was much the same as it was walking around town. Everyone wanted to shake his hand. He had his uniform on, washed and pressed, and he looked smart and respectable. The vicar read through the names of the boys who had been lost or wounded. By the time we walked out of the service, the bright eyed Bernie from breakfast was gone. The lost boy had returned. I dragged him off to the football field anyway. If anything can cheer our Bernie up, it's football. But even that didn't do the trick. He kicked the ball back at me with no enthusiasm. He looked around as if he was remembering, but not remembering the good times, only the sad.

"I'll go in goal," I suggested. "You can take some shots."

He picked up the ball. "No, I'll be the keeper, you can try to get one past me."

"You're not a goalkeeper," I said, reaching out for the ball. "You should work on your shooting while you have the chance."

"Why do you never want to take penalties?" he asked suddenly, as if he had been meaning to ask for years.

"It's not that I don't want to," I lied. "We don't have much time. We shouldn't waste it on me. I'll never play in a football match, there's no point."

"It's not because of that penalty shootout competition we had with Eric Longstaff all those years ago, is it?" I took the ball from him and walked towards the goal. "You know I never blamed you for missing that shot, don't you?"

"Are we playing or not?" I stood between the goalposts and kicked the ball out to him. He trapped it under his foot.

"It wasn't your fault." He kicked the ball at me with no real power. I lunged forward and stopped it, then kicked it back.

"You were really angry," I said.

"I wasn't angry at you. I was angry at Eric Longstaff and all those clowns in the crowd laughing at us. Angry that we were tainted by the workhouse, at Dad for going to prison and at Mum for leaving us there."

"It wasn't her fault. You know that."

"I know, but it didn't stop me from being angry at her. I was angry at the whole world." He kicked the ball with more force before I was ready, and it went through the net and into the bushes. I dashed after it, then kicked it high.

"I didn't help by missing that shot and losing the shootout. You should never have picked me."

He let the ball sail over his head, then ran to fetch it back. "Do you want to know why I chose you?"

"Because you thought I could do it. But you were wrong."

"No, well yes. I thought you could do it, but that's not why I chose you. I looked down the line of boys and there you were, with your arms folded and your head tipped back. Four-foot nothing ready to take on the world. I knew that if you missed the goal, you'd get over it. You could bear the loss. I knew it wouldn't break you. Even then you were so strong."

"But I let you down. I missed the goal."

"It was all down to luck, that's all. That's something I've learnt from the trenches. Taking penalties is a game of chance. Just like life. Just like war. I've seen some of the best soldiers, the fittest, with the brightest minds knocked over and killed while I stood right next to them unharmed. You could have trained every hour of every day and still missed. That's the way the world works." He dropped the ball and kicked it over to me. "I had a sergeant when we were training," he continued. "He used to say, *'Shoot lad, shoot. Pick your target and shoot.'*" Bernie smiled at the memory. "Of course he was talking about a different kind of shooting, but it's all the same. He said if you shoot ten rounds and hit once, that's all you need. But if you don't shoot any rounds, you definitely won't hit the target. Shoot lad shoot."

He picked up his jacket from next to the goalposts and we started for home. As he put it on his Viaduct Cup losers' medal fell out of his pocket.

The ribbon was still attached, but it was torn and filthy. I picked it up and handed it over.

"I don't know why you keep that old thing."

"It's my lucky charm, I suppose."

"It can't be that lucky. Doesn't it remind you of that day? Doesn't it remind you of losing?"

He ran his thumb over the surface. "It used to. It should still, but not now."

"You said it was a loser's medal. That it meant nothing."

"I did say that. But I was wrong. It means everything."

"If that was mine, I would have thrown it in the canal by now."

He smiled. "I wouldn't expect you to understand. How could you?"

"Why do you want to keep something that reminds you of the worst day of your life?"

"Because it wasn't the worst day of my life. Not by a long shot. At the time, I thought it was, but it was one of the best. This medal reminds me of that."

"But it's not the trophy, is it? It was always our dream for a Bracken to win the Viaduct Cup. To lift the trophy. To win the cup for Dad."

Bernie laughed. "I never wanted to win the cup for Dad."

"What do you mean?"

"Dad wanted to win the Viaduct Cup so he could prove to this town that he was nothing like his rogue of a father. Well, I wanted to win so I could prove I was nothing like my rogue of a father. I wanted to bury that pathetic workhouse boy once and for all. But things have changed. I've left that boy behind me now."

"Don't you want to win the cup anymore then? Don't you want to get your hands on the trophy?" I felt somehow betrayed, as if we had both had one dream forever and now Bernie was saying he didn't share it anymore.

"Oh, I will win the cup," he said. "One day I'll do it. But it isn't about the trophy. It was never about the trophy. This medal reminds me I was part of something. Something bigger than me. Something important. Playing for the cup was about achieving something with my pals, fighting for something against all the odds, together. Scoring a goal for your team is like nothing else in the entire world. It's special, to set your mind to something and work hard to achieve it. You'll never have a bond with any group of people like you do with those you have fought with, played with. This," he held up the medal, "reminds me that we tried. That me and Charlie and Beckett and Walter and Ronnie and Alf and all the others stood side by side and we tried. We were a team. No one can take that away from us. This medal reminds me of how we were."

CHAPTER 20

Dear Bernie,

I hope you are staying safe and well. We haven't heard from you for a while. The newspapers have reported on a big battle and some of the girls in the cutting room have had letters from the front. Please, could you write? Even just a line to let us know you are safe and well. Otherwise we will worry ourselves to distraction.

Your ever loving sister,

Kit

Dear Kit,

I am sorry I have not written sooner. I started a letter but missed the post, so I thought I'd as well wait and write some more. We've had a terrible time of it lately, but I hope we are now over the worst of it. We have a rest day tomorrow. But it doesn't mean rest. We'll repair the road, or clean the camp or saw wood for trench repairs no doubt. But at least we won't be in the thick of it for a while. A few of the lads are having a kick about, but I don't have the heart to join in, not without Charlie or Beckett. I never imagined when we signed up that we'd be still here two years later. I thought we'd be back playing in the cup final before too long. I'd have the chance to put right what I did wrong. I'd have the chance to win the cup for the Hatters. That day seems a million years ago now. I remember waking up with a dread in the pit of my stomach. I thought if we could dress you up as a boy and play you in our team we would win by a mile. You would have been our best player, Kit. You always were a better footballer than me. It came so naturally to you, your speed, your ball control, your understanding of the game. Such a shame you could never play in the proper matches. We were born the wrong way around you and me. I would never have made it to the cup final again if it wasn't for you, and I don't know if I ever thanked you for that. Well, I shall sign off now before I get too maudlin. Let me know your news. I like to hear about home, about the hatworks and Ned and the others. Even the smallest details keep the boys entertained. Could you send some more socks?

Ta ta for now,

Your loving brother,

Bernie.

Dear Bernie,

It was a relief to receive your letter and know you are safe. Here's my advice, I know you don't want it, but I'll give it to you anyway. Next time you're asked to play football- join in. It does no good to sit on the sidelines. Football is everything to you, and you mustn't forget that. You mustn't forget what it means to you. If you are feeling lost in the war, you can find yourself again on the football field.

Please write again soon. Stay out of trouble.

Your ever loving sister,

Kit

CHAPTER 21

The letter arrived on a warm day in early September. The letter that told us that our Bernie had been killed in the fighting. We had watched from the safety of our home as a cloud blew over from France and covered the town of Nether Bridge in darkness. All the boys had been in action at the front in July. The newspapers reported a glorious victory. They had gone over the top to overwhelm the enemy, take them by surprise and end it once and for all. But as the days passed, the price of victory became clear. The telegrams arrived in waves; it didn't seem real. More black armbands appeared, more young men reported dreadful wounds and even more would never come home at all. The bad news kept coming, Alf and

Fred and Bill and Les and Tony. But the telegram girl always walked past our door. Until that warm day in early September of 1916.

I should have stayed to comfort Mum but I couldn't. I ran. I ran along the muddy lane at the back of our house, through the sheets drying on the lines.

"Will you have a kick about with us Kit?" Little Andrew from next door and some of the neighbour's children were playing in the back passage. I had never turned down a game before, not even a scrappy scuffle in the street. But I didn't stop. I ran through the ginnel and up the cobbled road towards the park. Everywhere I looked I could see him, Bernie, laughing and joking, dribbling the ball down the street. I ran past Bamford Hatworks with the chimney still spilling out smoke into the layer of grime that forever sits above the town and on to the centre of the churned up football pitch at the Sidings. I lay on the grass, shivering even though it wasn't cold. I lay still for an hour or more before Ned lay down next to me. She was still in her maid's uniform with her coat over the top. She had come as soon as she heard.

"I knew you'd be here. Is it true? I heard

Martha Drysdale from the post office was at yours with a letter earlier? Is it Bernie?"

"Killed in action," I said, without getting up.

She didn't speak. There was nothing to say. She reached out and held my hand. We lay on the grass until the night drew in and the soft autumn smell of home fires overpowered the dirty smoke from the railway and the factories. We walked home together through the market square and along the road past the river. At the end of my street Ned took my hand. "Go home," she said. "Your Mum needs you. And you need her."

As I headed down the hill towards home, I stopped at the monument set back in the lane to the allotments. I'd never looked at it before, not properly. It was a cross on a plinth, engraved with one name:

'In memory of Captain Charles Carmody who fell in the Boer War, South Africa, 1901.'

Another boy of Nether Bridge killed in another battle far from home. I reached out to trace the letters of his name. Would they add Bernie's name to the memorial one day? I walked away, my head swimming with the idea of all those boys ending up as names on a piece of stone on the road to the allotments. Is that the way they would be remembered? The moment I walked in through the kitchen door, Mum grabbed hold of me and wept into my shoulder. I couldn't cry. I don't know why.

When Dad finally came home, drunk and singing, he took one look at our faces and knew. He read the letter and stumbled against the chair. I don't know if it was the shock or the drink that caused his legs to give way like that, but he took a breath and stood up straight. "That's that then," he said before turning and going out.

CHAPTER 22

After the letter, the days passed in a blur of the mechanics of life. We got up, we made the fire for tea, went to work, came home, went to bed. We didn't talk about Bernie. We didn't talk about anything much. Dad stayed away. We could tell he had been home a few times while we were at work because the kitchen was a mess and his dirty clothes were in the empty tin bath in the yard.

My patience wore thin. I was fined at work for being late and had to stay behind to redo some of my cutting. Mr Grimes said he would give me a second chance because of our Bernie, but the next time I wasted cloth it would come out of my wages. Not that I cared. I wanted everyone to leave me alone, but we had to get on with life as if nothing at all had happened.

I waited in the grocer's shop for an old lady to finish fussing over prices and weight measurements. Mum had sent me to get a pound of tea leaves and I couldn't go home empty-handed.

"Three packets of cigarettes for our John at the front," the woman said. The grocer placed them on the counter with her other goods. "No, make it two."

"That's three and six altogether." The grocer could see me scuffing the floor, willing things to move along.

"Are you sure that's a pound?" She held up the paper bag with the sugar in it. "Feels a little light to me."

"I weighed it out in front of you, Mrs Gunn, it's a pound alright."

I sighed and folded my arms. The woman looked back at me, but didn't take the hint to hurry.

"What boiled sweets do you have?" she asked.

"All you can see here?" The grocer gestured to the glass jars behind him.

"I'll take a quarter of barley sugars."

He took down the jar, weighed out the sweets, and poured them into a paper bag. "Is that everything?"

"Yes, I think so." He totted up the bill while she filled her basket. She took her time paying, but finally she left and it was my turn.

"Sorry to keep you," the grocer said. He didn't mean it. He was making a point that I was rude, huffing and puffing at the delay.

"Just a pound of tea." He didn't move. "Please." I added with a forced smile. As he turned to weigh out the tea, I noticed a packet of cigarettes on the counter, the packet Mrs Gunn had decided against buying for her son.

"That's one and six." He handed over the bag of tea and I gave him the money. As he turned to open the till, I put my hand on the packet of cigarettes, drew them off the counter, and slipped them into my pocket. I felt the old sensation that I remembered from the rag and bone round with my father. My fingertips tingled, and I smiled to myself.

"What was that?" the grocer asked, slamming the till drawer and turning back to me.

"What was what?"

"What did you just put in your pocket?"

"Nothing." I picked up my bag of tea and made

for the door.

"Hang on, what did you just put in your pocket. I saw you, what was it?"

"I didn't put anything in my pocket. You're seeing things."

"I don't think so. I know your sort. Let's have it!"

"You're mistaken mister," I said with a smile and reached out for the door. He leaned across the counter and grabbed my arm.

"Turn out your pockets. Do you want me to call the constable? If you haven't taken anything, you've nothing to hide."

"I will do no such thing," I said. The bell above the door rang as a customer came in. I took advantage of the distraction to pull my arm free. I pushed past the new customer and ran out into the street. As I ran, I looked back and saw the shopkeeper with his hands on his hips watching me go. I ran as fast as I could, filling my lungs and feeling my legs pumping fast and strong. I was laughing. I could have run for miles without tiring. I was free, powerful, independent. No one could tell me what to do. I stopped to catch my breath in the ginnel by the side of our row of terraces and leant against the wall. It was only when I stood up straight that the smile dropped from my lips. The feeling of freedom was gone, replaced by a heavy darkness. As I made my way towards our backyard, my legs felt like lead. My throat caught and tears ran down my face. Mum was in the kitchen, cooking at the stove. I didn't look at her. I put the bag of tea on the table, hung my coat on the hook in the hall and went straight up to my room. Lying on the bed, I stared at the ceiling. I was empty inside, just like the world was empty on the outside.

I must have fallen asleep because it was dark when I opened my eyes. There was a knocking on the front door. I knew it was Sergeant Beswick before I heard Mum answer. The only people to use the front door are the police and the rent man, and the rent wasn't due.

I sat against the wall at the top of the stairs.

"Stan's not here," Mum said.

"I'm not here for Stan. Where's your Kit?"

"Kit?" I could hear the surprise in her voice. Or was it disappointment? "Why?"

"I want to speak to her about an incident at the grocer's shop this afternoon."

"What incident?"

"Is she here or not?"

I hoped she would say I was out, but she didn't.

"Kit!" she called up the stairs. "Can you come down for a minute?"

I composed myself, brushed down my hair and swanned down the stairs as innocent as you like.

"Sergeant? How can I help?" I smiled.

"What happened at the grocer's earlier, Miss Bracken?"

"Oh, that? That stupid old man needs spectacles."

"What happened?" Mum asked.

"He accused me of taking something, stealing something. But I didn't."

"Stealing what?" I could see the muscles in Mum's jaw tighten. She knew I was lying. She always did.

"That's just it. He didn't know. Just thought he saw me put something in my pocket."

Sergeant Beswick took off his helmet and took out his notebook. "And you ran? Why would you run if you hadn't taken anything?"

"I didn't run. I left because he was accusing me of something I hadn't done. I know how it works. Just because I'm a Bracken, no one would believe me."

"So you deny it?"

"Of course I do. I spent good money in that

shop, and that's how he treats his customers. It's a disgrace."

Mum stepped forward, holding the doorframe, keeping the miserable policeman outside in the drizzle. "If that's all, I'll kindly ask you to stop harassing my family. I could make a complaint, you know."

"Mrs Bracken, I think we both know what's gone on here." He looked at me and replaced his helmet.

"Thank you Sergeant, let us know if you find out what went missing," Mum said, closing the door.

He stuck his foot out and stopped it from shutting, "I'm watching you, Kit Bracken. I know you're in league with your father's one man crime wave. It's only a matter of time before you slip up. And when you do, I'll be waiting."

I smiled and waved, showing the defiance against authority my father had taught me. I started singing, I couldn't help myself. "Goodbyeee, goodbyeee, wipe a tear baby dear from your eye-ee. Though it's hard to part I know, I'll be tickled to death to go." Mum closed the door on him, then looked at me with an expression that wiped the smile from my face.

"What did you do?" she hissed under her breath.

"Nothing. I swear. It was a misunderstanding."

"You sound just like your father." She reached into the pockets of my coat hanging on the hook in the hall and pulled out the packet of cigarettes.

"I just want to know why?" Mum asked as we sat at the kitchen table with the cigarettes in front of us. "You don't even smoke."

"I don't know why. They were on the counter and he wasn't looking and before I knew it, they were in my pocket."

"I thought you'd left all this behind you. I thought I could trust you. I hoped I could send you out for a pound of tea without bringing the police to our door."

"You can trust me. I'm sorry. It won't happen again. I wasn't thinking."

She reached across the table and held my hand. "We need to look out for each other now. I couldn't bear it if anything happened to you as well." I could see the worry etched across her face. I dropped my head. I felt terrible. This was the last thing she needed after Bernie.

CHAPTER 23

Of all the places in town, I felt closest to Bernie at the Sidings football ground. It should have been at home, or at the hatworks, where we had spent most of our time together, but it wasn't. Something about the Sidings connected me to him in a way nowhere else did. So I found myself there more often than ever before. It was a shadow of its old glory. The army had trampled the pitch, and they had left tent pegs and rubbish behind. The small terrace where we had stood to watch was abandoned; paint flaking off the railings, the wood beginning to rot. The goalposts still guarded either end, but the nets were torn and hung loose, flapping in the wind. I stood in the penalty box, Bernie's football at my feet. If I closed my eyes and concentrated, I could hear the crowd cheering, clapping and stamping their feet. I could hear the thud of the lads kicking the ball, the calls to pass, the crunch of heavy tackles. I could see Bernie and Charlie and Beckett and Walter and Alf and Ronnie, arms folded across their chests as the photographer from the Chronicle took their picture before the match. But when I opened my eyes, all I could see was the empty remains of what could have been. All I could hear was the thunder of a train shunting over the viaduct, blowing its whistle. The low hum of the factories and mills. A flock of jackdaws chacked in the trees. It wasn't fair. Bernie had one dream, and now it would never be. He wanted a Bracken to win the Viaduct Cup and now it would never be. I looked down at the ball and with a scream, I booted it through the open goal mouth. It flew towards the bushes, but before it was lost in the undergrowth, a foot stretched out and trapped it. A young woman reached down and picked it up.

"Good shot," the girl said, walking towards me.

"Thanks." I reached out for the ball, but she bounced it and rolled it underneath her foot.

"You're Kit Bracken, aren't you?"

An air of hostility came from her. As if we were sworn enemies and always had been, but I didn't know why. Perhaps she knew of our reputation in town. Once a Bracken, always a Bracken.

"Who wants to know?" I said, steeling myself for a fight. I recognised her from somewhere.

"It would have been a great day?"

"What would?"

"The cup final in 1914. Carmody Mill versus Bamford Hatworks. Carmody could have made history that day. They would have won the cup more times than any other team in history."

"Who's to say they would have won?" I asked.

She laughed. "It was a formality. Bamford Hatworks never had what it took."

"That team was the best we ever had. We would have won it the year before if it hadn't been for.."

"Oh yes. I remember now." She kicked the ball towards me. "It was your brother who got himself sent off, wasn't it? He attacked my brother for no reason."

"Your brother?" I picked up the ball. "Eric Longstaff is your brother?"

"Aggie Longstaff." She introduced herself. I

recognised her now. Of course, Aggie Longstaff. "I suppose we'll never know who would have won, but on the balance of history, we can assume it would have been Carmody Mill."

"You can't assume that." There was something smug about her. Something arrogant.

"Perhaps we can find out."

"Find out how? Toss a coin?" I laughed, but I wasn't laughing inside.

"No. We could play the game. Get a team together and we can play the match."

I stopped laughing. It was too good to be true. "No one will let girls play football," I said.

"Yes, they will. If it's for charity, they will. Carmody Munitions already has a team. Lord Carmody says it's great exercise for the girls, keeps us fit and healthy so we can work faster."

"Carmody Munitions have a football team?" She was lying, she had to be.

"We're not all that bad either. Take after our boys. We're looking for some teams to take us on. You should speak to Mr Bamford, get yourself a starting eleven."

"Mr Bamford will never let women play football."

"He might. If it's for charity he might, if it's for the Viaduct Cup, he might. I'm sure we can get a crowd, even if they are only there for the exhibition."

CHAPTER 24

I t took a few days to pluck up the courage to walk up the stone steps to the office. I waited for the final factory whistle to blow and for the hatworks to empty out. I hoped to catch Mr Bamford alone, but that would have been too much to ask. Ned was convinced he would say no. Old Mr Bamford was a Victorian man. He wore a suit with a pocket watch on a chain and top hat. He had wispy white mutton-chop whiskers on his ruddy cheeks and couldn't have been more old-fashioned if he tried. He was happy enough to have women working in his factory, (and to pay them half of what they pay the men, Mum said) but letting his women workers play football was another thing altogether. We had always played in the yard at dinner-time when the boys let us join in. But that was in fun. I was asking to play under his name. To represent Bamford Hatworks in front of the entire town. I knocked on the door and a voice called me in. Mr Bamford was sat behind his big old desk, scratching his chin, reading a letter. Miss Bamford, his daughter, was in the chair opposite and Mr Grimes stood to one side, ready to take the signed letters away.

"Kit." Mr Grimes ushered me out before I was even in the office. "What are you still doing here?"

"I wanted to speak to Mr Bamford Sir," I said.

"Well, you can speak to me. Tomorrow. On your way now."

"Let her in." Mr Bamford waved me in without looking up.

Mr Grimes didn't want to let me pass. "I'll see to this, Sir," he said pushing me out.

"She can come in." Mr Bamford looked up now. "Let no man… or woman… say I am unapproachable." He set down his letter and sat back in his chair, resting his hands over his bursting buttons.

Mr Grimes gave me a stern look and stepped aside. I stood in front of the desk, gripping my hat in my hands, which were suddenly clammy and cold. Miss Bamford moved her chair aside for me and smiled. Mr Bamford picked up the cigar from the ashtray in front of him.

"Well, what can we do for you Miss er...."

"Bracken," Miss Bamford confirmed, giving her father a disapproving look. He should know the names of his employees.

"Miss Bracken," he echoed.

This was my moment. I cleared my throat and looked at the expectant faces.

"Well Sir, Miss. With there being a war on and how we're all doing our bit. I wanted to see if we could do something for charity." I had prepared this much. I would mention the charity before the football.

Mr Grimes spoke up. "You can speak to me about this tomorrow. No need to disturb Mr Bamford, he's a very busy man."

"No, let her continue. How do you intend on raising money for charity?"

"Through football, Sir. We could arrange a football match, and we can collect money from the gate receipts."

There was a moment of silence. "That's a marvellous idea," Mr Bamford said at last. "You should speak to my daughter. You're raising money for an ambulance, that's correct, isn't it Hester dear?"

"Yes, father. That sounds like an excellent plan, Miss Bracken."

Mr Grimes coughed. "Might I ask how we would get the players? All the Bamford Hatworks team are at the front, or … not around anymore." He nodded to me in recognition of Bernie's sacrifice. "Unless we field a team of old men and young boys, who would we have to play? I don't think my knees would be up to the job," he laughed.

"That's just it, Sir," I said, swallowing. This was the moment I had been dreading. "It would be a team of ladies."

It's hard to explain how the atmosphere in the room changed when I said what I said. It was as if all the air had been sucked out of the window, even though the window was closed. Mr Bamford's face dropped, and he sat up. Mr Grimes coughed as if someone had punched him in the stomach. Miss Bamford widened her eyes and looked at her father.

"I beg your pardon," Mr Bamford said, daring me to repeat myself.

"W…Women. It would be a team of women. The Bamford Hatworks Ladies' football team."

He stood up now.

"Women do not play football!" He seemed taller than I had noticed before. "Women!" he raised his voice. "Do not play football."

"But they do Sir," I said, stepping back. "There have been matches played all over since the war started. I've read about it in the newspapers."

"It's true, father," Miss Bamford joined in. "I've heard about it. They've raised lots of money. Women do play football."

"Not in my name, they don't. As long as I live, there will never be women playing in my football team."

"But Sir…"

Mr Grimes grabbed my arm and pulled me towards the door. "That's enough. Come up with something else."

Before I knew it, I was back outside in the corridor.

Ned was waiting for me in the street outside.

"Well?" she asked.

"No chance." I walked on without stopping.

She followed me. "It was worth a try though, wasn't it? At least you tried." I don't know if I was more upset about not being able to play football, or not being able to beat Aggie blooming Longstaff. "We could play anyway, like you said. In the park."

"There won't be any match. It was a stupid idea."

As I walked away from the hatworks, I felt a burning inside my chest. Bernie had been denied his chance to lift the cup, and now I was being denied the chance to do it for him. Who were they to say we couldn't get our hands on that trophy? Why should we always miss out? Because they are rich and we are poor, because they are the employers and we're the workers? How is that fair?

CHAPTER 25

"So you're giving up at the first closed door?" Mum asked when I explained what Mr Bamford had said.

"What choice do I have? I can't start a football team by myself, can I?"

She was in the yard putting the sheets through the mangle. "Hang that up, will you?" She threw me a pillow case and began squeezing the water out of another. "I had dreams too, you know," she said. I looked through the sheets as I draped the pillowcase over the line in the passage. "Before I met your father."

"Dreams? What dreams?" I had never seen Mum as anything other than.. well, Mum.

"You needn't sound so surprised. I wanted to change the world too, in my own way," she shook her head. "My father was a union man. He was a shop steward," she explained. "I used to go with him to his meetings and help to write his speeches. We were fighting for better conditions for the workers and I was a part of that. I started going to some suffrage meetings and rallies as well."

"You were a suffragette?"

She laughed and turned the crank on the mangle. "We weren't called suffragettes then."

"Did you break windows? Go on protests?" I was impressed.

"I didn't go so far as breaking the law. The movement wasn't doing things like that back then, not that I would have, anyway. But I went to the meetings and on the marches, I wrote for the leaflets. I wanted to make a difference. I wanted to be a part of changing the world for the better. It didn't sit right with me that hard-working folk could be cast out through no fault of their own. I was fighting to have my say."

"Why did you stop?"

"I met your Dad. My father didn't approve of him. I think that was half the appeal. My dad was horrified that I might marry into the Bracken family, but I wouldn't be told. I left everything behind to be with your father. He thinks that his were the only dreams that were shattered that day on the football field, but it took from all of us."

"You could still do it. Have your say," I said. "You already speak for the women at the hatworks." Mum was always the first in line to stand up for the workers, to plead their cases if they were late or slow. She understood how hard it was to make ends meet and wasn't afraid to fight the masters.

"Unofficially."

"You could run as the union rep, for the National Federation of Women Workers."

"What do you know about that?" she asked with a smile.

"I've seen your pamphlets."

"Do you know something Kit? There are women in this street who used to tell me it wasn't right that I let you run around playing football with the boys. They said I should have stopped you, brought you in to the kitchen, told you to be more ladylike. But I could always tell you loved it and I didn't want to take away the one thing that made you happy. I know what that feels like. Now, I suppose, more than ever, we should go after our dreams. Don't give up just because the world is saying no. You'll regret it."

"But how can I?"

"You'll find a way. You always do."

CHAPTER 26

few days later, I saw Miss Bamford through the window of the Pavilion Tea Room in Victoria Park. I had tried to speak to her at work, but she was never alone. She sounded interested in the idea of a ladies' football team, and I thought perhaps she could persuade her father to let us do it. I hesitated as I stood outside the old Victorian glass house. I had never been inside before. It wasn't for the likes of us. The prices they charge are out of our range for a start, but the stuck up staff and well-to-do customers aren't exactly inviting. I've been out for tea before, of course I have, but we normally go to the tea shop in the market square or the one at the railway station. You don't have to get dressed up to go there. Mum did once buy me and Bernie an ice cream from the Pavilion. It was the day we went into the workhouse. She thought we should have a treat to take our minds off it, but we didn't go inside. Miss Bamford was at a table by the window. I took a deep breath and marched right in. The waitress blocked my way,

"Can I help you?" she asked with a sneer.

"I'm alright thanks," I said, brushing past her.

"We have a dress code in here." She followed as I walked into the dining room.

"I'm dressed, aren't I?" I said, spying Miss Bamford's table.

"No work boots," she said. "Do you have a reservation?" I ignored her and forged on. The glasshouse was decorated with exotic plants and elegant paintings. The tables were laid out with bright white tablecloths and vases of flowers. A woman in a long dress was playing fancy tunes on a piano. Some ladies taking tea at the other tables looked over as I hurried in.

"Miss Bamford, please can I talk with you?"

She looked up from her notebook with a cup of tea in her hand. "Miss Bracken," she looked at the waitress who was scurrying along behind, apologising for the intrusion.

"I'm sorry Miss, she just came right in."

"That's alright." Miss Bamford gestured for me to sit in the chair opposite. "What can I do for you?"

"I'm sorry to cause a fuss, but I wanted to speak to you on your own and this was the only place." I sensed that my time was limited. The waitress was hovering, ready to usher me away, so the words tumbled out.

"Take your time Miss Bracken, whatever is the matter?" I took a breath and Miss Bamford raised her hand for the waitress. "Could we get some more tea, please?" The waitress bobbed, gave me a filthy look, then went off to fetch the order.

"It's about the football Miss," I began. "I know the master said we couldn't have a women's team, but I don't think that's right. Other factories have women's teams and it's not indecent like they say, it's just football. They're raising lots of money for charities and I don't see why we can't too."

"I agree, but my father has put his foot down. I did try to persuade him. Between you and me I don't think he has a problem with women playing football, it's more that he doesn't want another losing team." She finished her tea and placed the cup on the saucer. "But you're right, this town has missed its football since the war started. We could have made a fortune from the gate receipts from a football match."

"And we still could."

"You heard what he said. There will never be a women's team playing under his name," she quoted her father word for word.

"That's why I wanted to talk to you. We don't have to use his name. We could start our own team." Miss Bamford raised her eyebrows then opened her mouth to speak, but at that moment the waitress came over with a tray of tea followed by a boy in a smart suit, bow tie and his nose in the air, carrying fresh cups and saucers. We waited for them to leave before saying any more. Miss Bamford sat forward to stir the pot.

"Do you mean a team that's completely separate from the hatworks?"

"Yes, our own team with our own name."

"I suppose we could do that." A rush of optimism washed over me. She said 'we.' A woman like Miss Bamford had influence. She was not used to people saying no to her. I could see the thoughts racing through her mind. "And really," she continued, "how capable a team would we get out of the workers at the hatworks? I mean no offence to the ladies at Bamford's, but I'm not sure they would be the best of the bunch. If we start our own team, we can select from the whole of Nether Bridge." She poured the tea, and we each took a cup.

"Yes, the whole of Nether Bridge. We could make a better team than any we could get from the hatworks." I agreed.

"All sorts of girls from town, not just hatters," she picked up her pen and opened her notebook. "My father couldn't object to that, could he?" she smiled. "It doesn't reflect on him at all."

"The only thing is Miss Bamford," I said, coming to my point. "I don't know how to do it. I can play football, I can teach others to play football, I'm sure about that. But I don't know how to get the kit together, how to find the players, how we'd be allowed to play at proper football grounds, I don't know how to arrange the matches."

"Well, I can take out an advertisement in the newspaper, I'll do it today." She turned her notebook to a fresh page and began writing a list. "When shall we have the selection day? Will Saturday suit?"

"Saturday? It would have to be in the afternoon, after work."

"I can root out the boys' jerseys from the

hatworks. Father can't object to that and once we have a team together, we can play at the Sidings." She looked up suddenly, as if a flash of inspiration had come over her. "Did you know that Carmody Munitions has a team? They play in their free time. I could speak to the old Lord and arrange a match against them."

I felt my heart quicken inside my chest. "That's a good idea."

"We could play for the Viaduct Cup!" She almost knocked her teacup over in excitement at the idea. "Imagine that? We could get the whole town out in support. We could advertise the game in advance and sell programmes on the day. The Viaduct Cup game has always brought out the crowds, even if people don't approve, I'm sure they'll still come to see what it's all about."

"Do you think Lord Carmody would allow that?"

"I can be very persuasive when I want to be Miss Bracken. I won't give Lord Carmody a say in the matter."

Dear Bernie,

I keep hoping it is all a terrible misunderstanding, but I know deep down it isn't. Mum is distraught. She carries on as she always does. She turns out for work and is strong for me and Dad, but I know her heart is broken. Last night I woke up to the sound of her sobbing through the wall. I climbed in bed with her and held her hand until she fell asleep. A lot has happened since I last wrote. I know you like to hear about what's gone on at home. I had a meeting with Miss Bamford at the Pavilion Tea room yesterday and I ran home excited to tell you my news. When I realised I couldn't, it was as if someone had thumped me in the chest. So I thought I'd write and tell you anyway. If we had a grave, perhaps I would come and speak to you there, but we don't, so this will have to do. I suppose you're wondering why I was taking tea at the Pavilion with Miss Hester Bamford? Bernie, you'll never believe it. We are to start a new football team! A ladies' football team. And I'm going to be the captain. Just like you. Miss Bamford said she will speak to Lord Carmody to arrange a match against his team of munitionettes. We might even get to play for the Viaduct Cup. If we do, I hope you will look down on us, to cheer us on.

Well, that's all for now. I have to prepare for the selection day on Saturday.

I think of you every day and I always will.

Ta ta for now,

Your ever loving sister,

Kit

CHAPTER 27

The Nether Bridge Chronicle

Wanted: Lady Footballers
Prospective lady footballers should attend a
selection session at the playing field in Victoria
Park, Nether Bridge at 2pm next Saturday.

CHAPTER 28

We were in the bandstand at two o'clock sharp. It was drizzling and still cold under the smog of the town. At ten past, no one had arrived.

"Give it a bit longer," Ned said. "It's Saturday afternoon. Most of them will have been at work all morning and then had chores at home. I suppose that's one thing the boys never had to worry about."

Esther Hart was the first to arrive. "I was looking for the football trials. Have I got the right day?" she said, looking around at the empty field, clutching her brother's football boots. Alice Croft, a clerk at the town hall, was next. Claudie Doyle from the greengrocers and Martha Drysdale from the post office, then Lucy Chadkirk arrived with Rachel

Cooper, a waitress from the tea shop at the station. Then my friend Ivy Winstanley from the hat shop and Freda Lane arrived on a bicycle. It was a disappointing turnout. I had fancied a selection day, choosing the best players plus some reserves for the team. But at this rate, we would be lucky to make a starting eleven.

"Right. Let's get on with it." I stepped forward, but Ned held me back.

"Kit, I was just thinking that… well…"

"What?"

"It's just some of these girls haven't played before, it's a big thing for them."

"It's a big thing for all of us." I didn't know what she was getting at.

"We want them to want to play. To be comfortable and confident."

"Of course we do."

"What I'm trying to say is…"

"What is it, Ned? Spit it out!"

"It's that. It's just that. The way you said that. I know you're passionate, but sometimes you can be blunt. Direct in the way you say things."

"We want to win this thing, Ned. It's not a tea party."

"I know. But we don't want to scare them off.

I'm just saying you should be gentle. Until they get to know you."

I gathered everyone around and stood on the first step of the bandstand. I would be gentle, as it was the first day.

"Thank you all for coming today. What we are planning to do won't be easy. There will be people who won't approve and some who will be willing us to fail, but from now on, we have to stick together. We are a team, a football team." Some of the girls clapped, pleased to have made the team without even kicking a ball. I looked down at the group of misfits. "Let's start by running round the field once to warm up, then we can do some passing."

I stood back as the girls began some drills. Most hadn't come dressed for the occasion. Their skirts and coats got in the way. I had long since learnt to hitch my underskirts up to free my legs, but I wasn't concerned. When we played for real, we would wear long shorts, just like the boys. There was some natural talent, but on the whole they were dreadful.

"It's the first time," Ned said. "Some of them have never kicked a ball in their entire lives."

"I know, but I expected better," I said as we watched on from the sidelines. "Use the side of your foot, Esther. Like this." I ran over and showed them again how to pass. "Trap the ball under your foot to control it, then pass it on. That's it."

"See, Esther's getting the hang of it," Ned said as I joined her. "They need some time, that's all."

I spotted Matilda Mossop, the stationmaster's daughter, hiding in the trees. I could see that she wanted to join in, but couldn't pluck up the courage.

"Matilda!" I shouted. "It is Matilda, isn't it?" I ran over and led her onto the grass. "This is Rachel," I introduced her to the chattiest member of the team. "Rachel? You know Matilda? From the station? Why don't you pair up and do some passing." At least now, we had our starting eleven.

After the warmup, I explained the rules, the basics, then we set ourselves up for a trial match. As we ran around in the mist, I noticed passers by stopping to watch. Some shook their heads in disgust. Two young soldiers home on leave tried to get involved.

"That's not how you do it. Let me show you. Here Wilf, let's show them how it's done."

They ran onto the field and took the ball from Esther's feet, then passed it between them both and scored a goal. It wasn't hard. Everyone stopped and waited for them to move on. "Come on ladies, you reckon you can play football. You need to get stuck in. Come on then?" He was mocking us.

His mate Wilf wasn't so keen. "Let's leave them to it, Lee."

"No, if they want to play football like the lads, they need to get stuck in like the lads."

I had seen enough. "Give the ball back. We're in the middle of a game."

"Call this a game?"

"We're training."

"Training my eye." Lee grabbed the ball. "It's ridiculous. Running around holding up their long skirts like that, how are they meant to get up any speed? Football isn't for girls. Leave it to the lads." He held the ball up.

"Give that back." I reached out for the ball, but Lee dropped it to his feet and rolled it away.

"If you're so good at football, come and get it from me!"

Wilf grabbed Lee by the arm. "Come on mate, let's leave them to it."

"No. I want to see what this lot can do. It takes all sorts of players to make a football team. And you haven't got any of them."

"Lee, mate, do you know who that is?" he said

under his breath. "That's Bernie Bracken's little sister."

Lee looked back, and his face dropped. "Here you go then." He kicked the ball softly to me. "No harm meant. We were only having a laugh."

I picked up the ball. "You'll be supporting us, I take it? The Allsorts football team? Spread the word."

The two lads nodded and scurried off. When they were out of earshot, everyone burst into laughter. We had the beginnings of a team.

Miss Bamford was waiting for us when the training session finished. She was sheltering from the rain in the bandstand, holding an umbrella.

"How about Christmas Day?" She couldn't keep the smile from her face.

"What's that, Miss?" I asked.

"The match. I've been to see Lord Carmody. He said he's already agreed to a team of his munitionettes playing for fun, for the distraction and exercise. He says it's good for them to stay healthy with the dangerous work they are doing, filling the shells with all the chemicals. So he only needed a little encouragement to let them play in a match."

The blood drained from my face. I looked at the mismatched players, laughing and joking as they walked away. We were bound to lose. We would be the laughingstock of the entire town. I could already see Aggie Longstaff's smug face gloating at our humiliating defeat.

"We've got plenty of time to sort ourselves out." Miss Bamford read my mind. "I'll get the boys' old jerseys from the hatworks and have them adjusted. We'll need some long shorts and caps. I'm not sure what we can do about boots, but we'll come up with something. Don't worry," she said. "The Allsorts football team will make an excellent account of themselves at the Viaduct Cup."

CHAPTER 29

Aggie Longstaff arranged a game against a team from Brinksway Spinners to try out their players. They advertised the match as a friendly and invited their workers along to support the girls. I heard about it from Martha, who had delivered a telegram to the munitions office and seen the poster on the wall. The Carmody Munitionettes, as they were calling themselves now, weren't wearing their boys' old jerseys. They turned out in a smart new kit; red blouses with a white bow at the neck and lovely bloomers to match. They were in long socks and it looked like they had new boots. I wasn't surprised. Lord Carmody spares no cost for his football team, men or women. There was a small crowd and they were charging a penny for entry. I paid the fee and stood with a group of workers from Carmody Munitions.

"Do you think they'll be any good?" One of them asked his pal.

"They should be. All the time off work they get for training. If I'd have known they'd get special treatment, I would have tried out for the team myself."

Time off work for training! That was something we could never organise. We were lucky to get everyone together, what with us all doing different jobs. The manager of the team was old Frank Fold. He'd been the successful manager of the boys' teams for almost fifteen years. He knew what he was doing. We didn't have a manager, not really. We couldn't count Miss Bamford because she didn't know much about football. Mr Fold called the girls into him with a whistle. They finished their warm up and gathered around him. There must have been twenty of them. Eleven players and almost as many in reserve. We struggled to make a starting eleven at all. When the match began, Carmody ran at the ball with intensity from the whistle. They were organised, passing across the pitch. Anytime one of the Brinskway girls got near, Carmody would chip the ball on to a waiting player. The way they ran rings around Brinskway, it was almost as if they had all twenty of them on the field. Carmody had a neat way of playing. Everything about them was neat; clean passes, organised formations. They knew where each other were on the pitch; they drew the defence away to create space and had so much time on the ball. I left when the halftime whistle blew. They were six nil up already. I didn't need to see anymore. I imagined the humiliation we would endure on the day of the cup match. How could we possibly beat a team like Carmody Munitionettes?

"You out think them. That's how," Mum said. "Sounds to me like they have a plan and they want to stick to it. So disrupt their plan. Ten to one, they won't know what to do if they're out of sorts." She smiled. "Maybe it's up to the Allsorts to put them out of sorts." She laughed at her own joke. But she was right. We might not have as many players or a smart new kit or an experienced manager, but maybe we could find our own style of play. To do that, we needed a friendly match. There was no way we could turn out at the cup final, having never played properly before. Miss Bamford agreed.

"I have a friend whose family owns a jam

factory in Upper Mill. He's just come home from a convalescent hospital after being wounded last year. He was very low when I went to see him. This might just be the perfect project for him to get his teeth into."

CHAPTER 30

The Allsorts met at Nether Bridge railway station for the short train journey to Upper Mill and the field where we would play our first match. We were full of nerves and excitement. Would there be a crowd? Would we play well? Maud Smith, the captain of the Albion Conserves team, greeted us at the station and walked with us down to the field.

"This is all very exciting," she giggled. "We've been rehearsing all week. Not that we're any good, but it's all in good fun, isn't it? It's for charity, for the war effort, and that's the main thing."

"Hopefully the gate receipts will be generous," I said.

"Even if it is folk coming to see the spectacle of women trying to play football," she laughed.

"But we can play, can't we? We might not be as good as the boys, we don't have as much experience as them. But we can play."

"That's what I said to the girls when I put the poster up. I don't know about you, but I had a hell of a job getting a team together. It's touch and go whether some of them will turn up today."

I felt my confidence growing. Maybe we would have a chance at winning. It would be the boost the girls needed before the big game.

"Albion Conserves? You make jam?" I asked.

"Jam for the boys at the front. I thought about leaving, going to work in munitions, doing something with a direct impact. But then a lad from our church came home and said how important the jam is to them out there. A taste of home he said. Who'd have thought a tin of jam could mean so much? But it does. So that's why I stayed on. What do you do?"

"I work in the hat factory. We make hats for the uniforms, and the tin helmets now too."

"I suppose we're all playing our part. Here we are. This is the field. Through there is the visiting changing room. Let me know if you need anything.

We'll see you on the pitch." We shook hands, and she jogged away. I had imagined our opposition as the enemy, but they were just like us.

Miss Bamford arrived in the motor and distributed the kit. It was clean, and pressed. She had brought some mob caps for us to wear, and belts so we could tie the shorts tight. We looked smart. We looked like a proper football team.

The weather was against us, so we didn't draw much of a crowd. But the eyes of the few people on the sidelines were enough to unsettle us. We missed passes and scuffed our kicks. The Albion team were in the same state. We scored first. It resulted from a corner. I sent it in low and found Martha, who pulled the ball away from the Albion defenders and teed up a shot on goal. She chipped it in off her left foot and it went in uncontested. We celebrated as if we had won the cup already. The Allsorts first ever goal settled us. We knew what we had to do. We had done it before and we could do it again. No more hoofing the ball or aimlessly running up and down the pitch. We went into the break a goal ahead. The changing room was a gaggle of excitement as we re-enacted the goal. It was as if we had come off stage; the adrenalin pumping through our bodies. But the optimism didn't last long. Their equaliser came in the first five minutes of the second half. The Albion players were delighted. Like us, it was their first ever goal. I couldn't begrudge them that. Their second goal was unforgivable. We lost concentration and let the Albion forwards run away from us. I screamed at Ned to send in a tackle, but she was too slow on the turn. Claudie was looking into the crowd and let the ball pass through her legs. "Pay attention!" I shouted as I ran to defend. I couldn't do everything myself. The Albion centre forward found herself in our goalmouth, one on one with our keeper. She stopped and couldn't make a decision. Should she shoot or dribble past our goalie? Should she wait for support from her team and send in a cross? By the time we arrived to defend, she'd had all the time in the world. She sidestepped our goalie and tapped the ball into the back of the net.

"What was that?" I shouted. "Where were you? Matilda, you're meant to be playing in defence. You were away with the fairies."

"Sorry, I didn't realise," Matilda said, walking away.

"Well, you need to switch on. Same goes for

everyone else. That was pathetic. Think about what we did in training. It's not good enough!" I felt a dread bubble up inside me. How would we ever win the cup if we played like this?

"Alright Kit. Calm down." Ned ran back to the centre spot next to me. "We're doing our best. We've never played before, remember."

"I don't know why we bother if this is the best we can do."

We played on for a further forty minutes, but we couldn't break through their defences. In the dying minutes, a sliding tackle brought Martha down just in front of the goal, and the referee awarded a penalty. The Allsorts gathered round, and I picked up the ball. We had a chance to equalise, to get back in the game.

"Should we stand behind you, Kit?" Martha asked. "In case it rebounds off one of their defenders?"

"No," I said. I looked around at the crowd. Suddenly they weren't the jam factory workers or the people of Upper Mill. They were the crowd cheering on Eric Longstaff in the penalty shoot out all those years ago. I could hear them ridiculing me as I missed and fell onto the frosty ground. I saw their laughing faces. My mouth went dry, my heart beat against my eardrums, my hands went cold. "I think you should take it, Martha," I held out the ball and she took it reluctantly.

"I can't take it."

"Yes, you can. I know you can do it." I turned away.

"But I haven't prepared for this. I haven't done it before."

"It doesn't matter. Just aim for the goal."

"But shouldn't you take it?" She followed me as I walked away. "You're our best player, our captain. You know what you're doing."

I turned. "I'm the captain and I know what's best. You need to take it. You can do it, Martha. I wouldn't ask you to do it if I didn't think you could."

Martha walked back towards the referee with her shoulders down. She might score. There was always a chance. The ball slammed straight into the goalkeeper and bounced back into play. We lost the game two goals to one.

CHAPTER 31

I arranged an extra training session in the week before the big match. I had some notes, some ideas to try out with the team. Miss Bamford turned up to give us all some tickets for our families.

"You all played marvellously against Albion Conserves. I thought we'd equalise with that penalty, but it wasn't to be."

"We should have scored from that," Claudie said, folding her arms.

Martha shuffled in her seat. "I tried my best. I didn't know I was expected to take the penalties," she said, clearly still upset from her miss.

Ned spoke up. "Wouldn't it have been better if

you'd taken the shot, Kit? You're our best player and no one else has trained for penalties."

"That's why we had a friendly match. So we know what to work on," I explained.

"You should have warned us." Martha folded her arms. "I didn't have a clue what I was doing. All those people watching on. It was embarrassing."

"I'm sorry, but that's football. We weren't good enough. We must do better if we want to be in with a chance at winning the cup."

"We did our best, Kit. It didn't help with you shouting at everyone all the time. You said we needed to build confidence for the big game, but our confidence is at rock bottom now."

"Martha's right," Claudie agreed. "I'm not sure I even want to play if it's like that. I ran my heart out on that pitch."

"We lost," I said. "That's the bottom line. It doesn't matter how hard we think we've played if we lose."

"We can't win every game, Kit. That was our first ever match, remember." Claudie looked round at the rest of the team who nodded in agreement.

Martha stood. "If we had to win, why didn't you take the penalty?" She wasn't letting it go.

"I thought you were going to take it, Kit,"

Claudie said. "You took the ball, but then you passed it to Martha."

"It was a tactic. They would have been expecting me to take it. We should all be able to do everything."

"Seemed to me like you bottled it," Martha said.

"I didn't bottle it! It was our opportunity to try things out, see who can do what."

"Well, you can count me out. Find yourself another mug." Martha picked up her coat and stormed out of the changing room.

"Where are you going?" I called after her. "I didn't mean to show you up."

"I don't think Martha sees it that way. She thinks she lost it for us and you put her in that position, in front of a crowd. It wasn't fair really, that's what I think." Claudie picked up her bag and followed Martha out.

"Great! How can we play in the final a player down?" Ned asked.

"I'll talk to her." I made to follow, but Miss Bamford held up her hand.

"Let me. I'll go after her. Might I remind everyone here that we are the Allsorts football team and if we don't act like a team and play like a team, then it won't matter a jot who takes the penalties."

"Some team," Ned said. "We don't have a team if Martha won't play."

"Well, I'm not playing if we're one down." Matilda made for the door, followed by several others, who muttered in agreement.

"No! Come back," I called after them. "We can't give up now. The match is only a few days away. We have to get some training in," I pleaded.

"Looks like you're on your own, Kit." Ned shook her head in disappointment and left.

CHAPTER 32

Dad never needed an excuse to get drunk, but Bernie's death was as good an excuse as any. Anyone would think Bernie's loss was his and his alone. The package didn't help. A brown paper parcel was delivered to our door on Christmas Eve. We looked at it unopened on the kitchen table until Dad came home.

"What are you waiting for?" The booze reeked on his breath and he didn't take any care with the precious package. He ripped open the paper, and the contents spilled onto the floor. It was all the things Bernie left behind in the trench; his spare clothes, books, letters and rations. Mum knelt down to pick up a shirt. She held it to her as if Bernie were still wearing it. I grabbed his notebook before it was torn in the scuffle I knew was about to break out.

"Why did you let him go?" Dad spat at mum, sweeping the rest of Bernie's mud caked clothes from the table.

"I didn't let him go, Stan. He was doing his duty. He had no choice." The tears rolled down Mum's face, but she made no sound of crying.

"But you didn't stop him Elsie, you waved him off. I saw you."

"I had to be strong for him. He didn't want to see us crying, did he?"

"Fetch me a drink." He slammed his hand on the table. "Fetch me a drink I said!" His chair scraped on the stone floor as he reared up.

"We don't have any drink in the house, Stan. You know that. Not after you signed the pledge."

"You're going to throw that in my face now? The pledge? You expect me to keep to the pledge when I've lost my boy? My boy." He reached out for Mum and pushed her against the stove.

"Stan, Please!"

"Dad don't!" He looked startled, as if he had only just noticed I was there. He let go of Mum and lunged for me.

"Will you fetch your old man a drink, Kit?" He stumbled against the table. "It helps to ease the pain of losing my boy." Then he slumped into the old armchair in front of the fire and sobbed.

Mum wiped her eyes. "Let's have some tea," she picked up the old cast-iron kettle.

"I don't want tea, woman!" Dad hauled himself to his feet. "Why don't you understand me? Why have you never understood me?" He grabbed the kettle from her hands and threw it across the room, the water spraying the walls. It clattered against the floor and came to rest under the table. The noise ignited Dad's rage. He pulled over the armchair and swept his arm across the pots and pans on the stove. Mum reached out for me and together we hurried into the yard. We pulled the kitchen door closed behind us.

"Let's go," Mum said. "Leave him to calm down. We can go into town for tea, then head up to church for midnight mass. How does that sound?" She was breathless, holding steady when she was anything but.

I glanced through the kitchen window as we left. Dad was crying and hurling cups and plates against the floor. He stopped, took down the photograph of Bernie and sank to his knees.

. . .

After tea, I left Mum in town and walked over to the post office. I wanted to clear the air with Martha. I couldn't risk her not showing up for the match. If she decided not to play, we wouldn't have enough players to make up our team. It would mean certain defeat and humiliation, and I could see the others refusing to play if Martha didn't show. If I was completely honest, I wouldn't blame them. I found her getting her bicycle ready to go out to deliver a telegram.

"I'm busy," she said, turning her back on me.

"I wanted to apologise. I was in the wrong. I shouldn't have asked you to take that shot."

"No, you shouldn't." She put the telegram in the bag at her side.

"You were right. I lost my nerve. It won't happen again."

"No, it won't because I'm not playing."

"Martha, please. You have to. We need you."

"I felt terrible after that match. Why would I keep doing something that made me feel so bad? I'm not stupid."

"It won't feel like that again. Not if we win."

"And what if we don't? Carmody are a better

team than the Allsorts. It'll be the same all over again, except with a bigger crowd and more expectation. If you were screaming and shouting at everyone in a friendly, I can't imagine what you'll be like in a cup game."

"I won't scream and shout. I promise. I was wrong. It was my first match too. I didn't know what to do. Please play. We're a team and you're a part of the team."

"I'm sorry." She climbed on to her bicycle.

"Will you think about it? Please Martha, we need you."

"I have a telegram to deliver." I watched her cycle away.

CHAPTER 33

S o that was that. It was all over before the referee had even blown the starting whistle. The match would be nothing but a humiliating defeat. Aggie Longstaff was right all along. We'd set ourselves up to fail again. I half wondered if I should fake an injury to get out of it. Maybe I could throw myself down some steps and get myself a real injury. The day that I had waited for my entire life was almost upon us, and the feeling of excitement in my stomach turned to a feeling of dread. I rushed for home through the foggy streets. I wanted to get into bed and forget about everything. But I found myself walking in through the gates of the Sidings football ground. Someone had mown the grass and painted out the white lines.

The torn nets had been patched together with tape and the rubbish and leaves swept away from the seating area. I couldn't understand why I was drawn to this place. It had been the scene of so much pain and heartache. There was something about it though, dreams were shattered here, but they were also made here. Perhaps it was the possibility that kept me coming back, this place that said there was always a chance. But not this year. Not for me. I peered in through the door to the changing room, familiar with its damp smell and peeling paint. As I passed the referee's room, a sparkle caught my eye through the window in the door. The Viaduct Cup trophy sat on top of a cabinet, they had brought it down from Carmody Mill ready to present to the winning side. Someone had already tied the coloured ribbons of each team to the handles, green for the Allsorts and red for Carmody Munitions. I imagined myself standing with my team, raising the cup. But I couldn't help seeing an alternative image of Aggie Longstaff smirking as Lord Carmody shook her hand and awarded her the trophy. I can't explain it. I wasn't thinking. If I'd thought about it, it wouldn't have happened. But I wanted that trophy and it was right there in front of me. I deserved that cup; it had been taken from us too many times. I looked around to make sure I was alone, then I used my elbow to break a little square of glass in the door of the referee's room. Then I reached in and lifted the latch. The trophy was in my bag within seconds.

I ran in through the kitchen door and called out to say goodnight. The kitchen was still a mess after Dad's tantrum earlier on. Mum had picked up the kettle and brushed some of the mess to the side. Bernie's uniform jacket was hanging over the back of one of the chairs and his notebook was open. He had written scores from card games and accounts of how much of his wages he would send home to Mum. There was a list of items he needed, socks and shirts and boot laces. I went up to my room, put the chair against the door then sat on the bed and pulled back the canvas flap of my bag. The silver trophy with its ribbons attached looked much less impressive in my dirty old bag than it had in the referee's room. I looked in the mirror on the back of the wardrobe and held it up. Finally, I was lifting the Viaduct Cup, the actual Viaduct Cup. But no one would ever know. I couldn't show it off. I had the cup, but I hadn't fought for ninety minutes on the pitch with my team to win the match. I saw Bernie's face in the photograph on my bedside reflected back at me. There was a look of disapproval in his eyes. I let the trophy fall into my lap, it felt like a worthless piece of tin in my hands. "I don't want it," I said out loud to myself. "Not like this. It's not about the trophy. It was never about the trophy!" I threw it onto the bed. The moment they discovered the cup was missing Sergeant Beswick would be at our door. I had dreamt of holding the cup for years and now I couldn't wait to get rid of it. I had to replace it, put it back. I put the trophy back into the bag and made my way downstairs. As I opened the kitchen door a thick black smog reared up in front of me. The fog had mixed with the smoke from all the home fires on such a cold night and I could barely see my hand in front of my face, so I determined to go in the morning. I would wake up early and replace the cup at the Sidings before anyone noticed.

I didn't have any trouble waking up early; I didn't sleep at all. I lay on my bed with the trophy under the covers, it felt hot against my legs, so despite the frost cracking the windows, I didn't feel cold. As soon as I saw the first lightening of the sky outside, I was up. The smog had cleared a little, but the temperature had dropped. I shivered as I opened the kitchen door so I pulled Bernie's uniform jacket from the back of the kitchen chair. It was filthy, covered in dried mud and smelt damp and mouldy but I put it on. It was too big, of course, but it was heavy and warm and the last person to wear it was my brother. I pulled my coat over the top, drew my hat low to cover my face, and went out into the early morning. The town was as quiet as I had ever seen it. No trains or factories or motor cars. Dogs barked in back yards as I made my way through the streets. I didn't dawdle; I wanted to get rid of the trophy and be back in bed before anyone knew I had been out.

CHAPTER 34

As I approached the football ground, I heard voices, so I leant against the wall and listened in.

"Sorry to bring you out so early Sergeant." It was Frank Fold, the manager of the Carmody Team.

"And you're sure it was in here?"

"I brought it here myself yesterday afternoon," Mr Fold explained. "I didn't want to have to go back to the office to fetch it this morning. I wanted to focus on the match."

"The door wasn't locked?"

"It was definitely locked when I left. What I don't understand is who on earth would want to steal a trophy? It has no value, not financially."

"I have a few ideas about that," Sergeant Beswick said.

I backed away. It was too late. I couldn't put it back. I couldn't undo what I had done. I wandered down to the river and sat on the bank underneath the viaduct with the trophy at my feet and worked through my options, it didn't take long, there weren't many. I could get rid of the trophy, throw it in the river. No one need ever know. But I couldn't do that, not to the Viaduct Cup. I could hide it and deny all knowledge of its disappearance. If Sergeant Beswick had no evidence, he couldn't arrest me, could he? But he could make life very difficult. Even if he couldn't prove it, Mum would know. She could see right through me. My thoughts turned to Bernie. At least he would never know. I couldn't have taken that shame. I shivered and as I pulled Bernie's jacket around me, something hard dug into me from the inside pocket. I reached in and pulled out his Viaduct Cup loser's medal. I rubbed my fingers across it, imagining it in Bernie's hands. Then I put it over my neck and let it hang against my heart. Also in the inside pocket was an envelope. I held it up. It had my name on the front, with our full address, as if Bernie had meant to post it, but never had the chance. A lump caught in my throat. It was his last letter, but he didn't know it. There was a part of me that didn't want to open it, because once it was read, I would never hear anything new from Bernie ever again. But I couldn't wait. I carefully opened up the envelope. The letter was dated the day he was reported killed:

Dear Kit,

I hope you are keeping well and staying out of trouble. Sorry I haven't written for a while, we've joined up with another battalion whose numbers have been cut by the fighting and we've been busy showing them our way of doing things. We've had some quiet nights recently and there are a few things that have become clear to me out here.

Last week I was on sentry duty with Eric Longstaff. The nights on the fire step are long and we got chatting. Kit, I got him all wrong. He said he was always scared of me. That's why he fronted up and challenged me. He wanted me to think that he was tough, so I would leave him alone. But he's not tough. I thought the entire world was out to get me, because I'm a Bracken. That's what Dad always said. I thought the town was waiting for me to fail, willing me to fail. Eric told me he didn't mean to kick me in the face at the cup final. He said it was an accident, and I believe him. He doesn't have it in him to do something like that on purpose.

Well, it's just dawned on me that if he wasn't out to get me, if he didn't target me, then I pushed him for no reason. I deserved to be sent off. I thought I wanted revenge. But it wasn't revenge that I needed because it was no one else's fault. It was all down to me. What happened that day was no one's fault except my own.

You're right when you say that I shouldn't sit on the sidelines. Next time there's a kick about, I'll join in and do some training, so when we replay that match I can do it right. When this is all over, and I'm playing in the final of the Viaduct Cup, I'm going to wear that losers medal around my neck and take responsibility. I won't blame anyone or anything else for what I do. I'll remember the boys we lost and do them proud.

Well, I've volunteered to run a message back to battalion HQ, so hopefully I can get a hot meal and a warm bed before I have to come back to my unit.

Could you please send me some more stamps so I can write to Mum. Please thank her for the cigarettes.

Sending all my best wishes to you and Mum and Dad.

Ta Ta for now,

Your loving brother,

Bernie.

I read the letter twice before carefully folding it and putting it back in my pocket. I had a sudden urge to write back to him. To tell him I would look after his medal. I wanted to let him know that although he couldn't play in the cup final, I could, I would do it for him. And I would do it the right way. I would persuade Martha to play. I had to. And if she wouldn't, we would play with ten, win or lose, we would do our best. I clutched the medal around my neck. Funny how his loser's medal meant more to me now than the actual trophy. Something struck me. I didn't care if I won the Viaduct Cup or not as long as I could play. I couldn't let my teammates down. They would expect me to be there with them. To lead them. I had to be a part of it. But then I looked down at the trophy and realised that it was too late for all that. I took a deep breath and stood up. I could picture the smug expression on Beswick's face when I told him what I had done.

Maybe I could plead with him to let me play, to deal with the theft after the match, but he had been waiting for his moment far too long to be lenient. And why should he? I deserved everything that was coming my way. But my team didn't deserve it. Mum didn't deserve it, and neither did Bernie.

The street outside the football ground was busy. It was the event the town had been waiting for. A shiver went down my spine. The silver band was playing Christmas carols and collecting money for charity. The war might have reached a third Christmas with no end in sight, but for today at least, the war was forgotten. As I rounded the wall outside the ground I stopped as I spotted Sergeant Beswick. He had his arms behind his back, speaking to Lord Carmody.

"Don't worry, M'lord. It's just a matter of time." He scanned the crowd as they entered through the turnstiles.

"And you're sure you know who the culprit is?"

"I have a fair idea, M'lord, yes."

"I don't know what the world is coming to, Sergeant. Who would do such a thing?"

"Someone with no scruples, that's who."

I took one last look around at the excited crowds, the frosty grass on the pitch, waiting for the battle to begin. I saw some of the girls from the team making their way into the home changing room. Ned and Rachel and Ivy waved to the supporters and giggled nervously. There was no sign of Martha. I wasn't surprised. A wave of sadness washed over me. Only hours ago, I wanted to find a way out of playing in a lost cause and now I had my wish. I adjusted the bag in my hand with the trophy weighing heavy and stepped forward to admit my guilt and face the consequences.

CHAPTER 35

"**R**eady for your humiliation?"

I jumped as Aggie Longstaff appeared at my side.

"What?" I closed up the bag and tucked it in beside me.

"On the pitch. Are you ready for the Carmody girls to beat your rag-tag bunch of misfits?"

"Oh right. Yes." I looked over, distracted by Sergeant Beswick who was on his tiptoes scanning the crowd.

"Yes?" Aggie was confused.

"I mean no." My heart skipped at least three beats as I saw the smirk grow across Beswick's face as he spotted me and started towards us.

"Are you alright?" Aggie asked.

"I've done something," I said, looking down at the bag. "Made a mistake." There was no point lying, not anymore. She'd find out soon enough. Everyone would. Aggie looked at me and then at Beswick, who called out my name.

"Miss Bracken, I'd like a word."

I felt the entire football stadium heave in at the corners. Aggie stepped in front of me, blocking out the sight of Beswick as he pushed his way through the crowds. "Give it to me," she said.

"What?"

"Whatever you've got, give it to me and I'll sort it."

"I don't understand."

She looked over her shoulder and held out her bag. "Hurry, there isn't time. Whatever is in that bag, give it to me, give it to me now." I could see Beswick getting closer, so I did as she instructed. She took my bag with the trophy inside and I took hers. As soon as we had made the swap, she turned and walked past the policeman towards the changing rooms. Beswick reached out for my arm as if I was about to run, but I wasn't going anywhere.

"I've been waiting for you," he smiled as he took Aggie's bag from my grip. "Where is it then? Not singing now, are you?" He led me to the side and opened up the bag. He rifled through the contents. There were clothes and a hairbrush, a notebook and a pair of football boots. "Hidden it, have you?"

"Sergeant, I…"

"Shall we go back to your house? I suppose I'll find it under your bed. You can deny it all you want…."

"I'm not…"

"Miss Bracken, when the one thing that everyone knows you covet more than anything else goes missing, you should expect the spotlight to shine on you." He closed the bag, took me by the elbow and began to escort me from the football ground.

"Sergeant?" a voice called from behind. "Sergeant!" Beswick turned as Lord Carmody held his silver topped cane above the crowds, which parted to let him by.

"Ah, Lord Carmody. We'll soon have this unpleasantness sorted out."

"There's no need. I'm terribly sorry that we bothered you, but it turns out there's been an embarrassing misunderstanding. The trophy isn't missing at all. My man must have left it in the changing room, not the referees room where he said it was."

"You mean you've found it?"

"I mean, it was never missing at all. I am so sorry to have made such a fuss." He reached into his inside pocket, pulled out his wallet, and handed over a note. "Here, why don't you and the boys have a Christmas drink on me and Lady Carmody. To thank you for all your efforts. Good man," he added as he turned and made his way back to his guests in the stands.

Beswick gritted his teeth and let me go with a push. "Looks like it's your lucky day. On your way."

I didn't wait around to be asked again; I took Aggie's bag and ran for the safety of the changing room.

CHAPTER 36

"Where have you been?" Ned said as she threw me a jersey. As I sat to dress, I looked around at the team and sensed the nervous excitement rippling through them. Ivy was tying her shoelaces. She tied them once, then doubled the knot, then she undid them and started again. Ned tucked her jersey into her shorts and closed her eyes. Her hands gripped the sides of the wooden bench. As I looked at each player in turn, my eyes settled on Martha who was standing in front of the mirror, clipping her hair under her cap. She caught my eye in the reflection and nodded. I nodded back and looked away with a smile. Maybe, just maybe, we could win the cup after all.

We ran out onto the pitch with our green and white striped socks pulled up high and our caps straight and sturdy. Mum was waiting for me on the sidelines. She had a stack of leaflets in her bag and as a group of women from the hatworks walked past, she handed them out, "Can I count on your vote on Wednesday ladies? Elsie Bracken for NFWW Union Rep. We deserve better conditions and I will fight for your rights. Elsie Bracken, remember my name."

"How could we forget?" one of the women said as they took the leaflet and shook her hand. "You can count on our vote."

"Thank you, ladies. I won't let you down," she said as she turned to me. "You left early?"

"I wanted to be ready," I said, looking down. Did she know what I had done?

She smiled. "Look at you. So smart in your kit." She straightened my cap and flattened down my collar. I could see that she was trying to keep her emotions in check, her shame in check. She noticed the ribbon around my neck and pulled out Bernie's medal. She grasped it in her hand and then tucked it carefully back under my jersey, then put her hands on my shoulders. "I just wanted to say…" She looked down.

"Mum, I…"

"I just wanted to say," she cut me off, "how very proud I am of you." She looked me in the eye. "I know how hard you have worked for this. I know how difficult it is for you, after everything. It takes courage to do what you're doing. It's inspiring."

I looked away. I couldn't lose my focus now, not when the match was minutes away. "Our Bernie thought the world of you," she said. "And I know.." she swallowed, "I know that he's looking down on you and cheering you on. Whatever happens today, you've done him proud already. You've done me proud already."

We lined up next to the Carmody team while the silver band played God Save the King. The vicar read out a sermon and we all gave a moment's silence for the fallen of our town. The mayor tossed the coin and Aggie chose which end to start. I could have been mistaken, and it might have sounded different from the pitch, but the crowd appeared bigger and louder than any match Bernie had played in. I stood in the centre spot opposite Aggie and waited for the referee to start the match.

"Why did you do that?" I asked.

"Do what?"

"You know what. Why would you help me like that?"

"Because if this is to be any kind of contest, the Allsorts will need their best player on the pitch. When we beat you, I want us to beat you at full strength, fair and square. There's nothing more to it than that."

"Well, thank you," I said, holding out my hand. "But don't think I'll go easy on you in the game."

"I wouldn't expect anything less," she smiled and shook her head. "Good luck," she said, taking my hand. I opened my mouth to return the sentiment, but before I could she added, "you'll need it." The referee blew the whistle and Aggie shoved me out of the way. The match began.

CHAPTER 37

I won't go into detail about the first half. We were a mess. We couldn't get ourselves together. Maybe it was nerves or the unfamiliar sensation of being watched by such a loud and earnest crowd. The shouts were unsettling. There was a general roar of noise, but we could make out individual comments.

"Kick it! Don't tickle it!"

"My granny could play better than this lot!"

"What a load of rubbish!"

"Your goal is the other end, love!"

"Shame on you!" a man shouted. "No place for a woman." which was funny from someone who had paid to watch the match.

But as I stood at the corner flag, I heard a man say, "Football is football no matter who's playing. And I've missed it. Come on, you Allsorts!"

At half time we were two- nil down. As we ran in, Dad was waiting for me outside the changing room. I was surprised to see him, I didn't think he'd show up after his performance the night before, but he wouldn't have missed a Viaduct Cup match. He waved me over. His cheeks were hollow and the silver stubble on his face told me he had stayed out all night. I could smell the gin coming through his pores and his eyes were yellow and bloodshot.

"You know what's happening here, don't you?" he said.

"What do you mean?"

"That referee, he's a disgrace."

"What?"

"He's on their side. Some of those decisions were criminal. That was definitely a free kick to you outside their box."

"The referee is a neutral Dad, he's not even from Nether Bridge."

"There's no such thing as a neutral referee. They can all be bought. The same thing is happening all over again. It happened to me, it happened to Bernie, and now it's happening to you. As soon as they saw the Bracken name on the team sheet, you were on to a loser. It was all decided before you even set foot on the pitch."

"No Dad. It's not like that."

"They won't let you win the trophy. They'll never let a Bracken win the cup, that's a fact and we have to accept it, sooner or later we'll…"

"Stop it Dad!" I'd heard enough. He stepped backwards in surprise and held onto the wall to keep his balance. "This has nothing to do with being a Bracken. They're two nil up because they played better than us. It's as simple as that."

I left Dad to his self pity and joined the others in the changing room. It was freezing, but we didn't notice the cold through our exhaustion. We sat in silence, catching our breath. The Carmody Munitionettes team next door were chanting and clapping and stamping their feet. They were cheering as if they had already won. Miss Bamford handed out cups of water. I shook my head and looked around at the shattered bodies. I had to do something.

"Why are you here?" I asked. A sea of confused faces looked back at me.

"We're here to win the cup, of course. What do you mean why?" Martha asked.

"Why did you answer the advert in the newspaper to join a ladies' football team?"

Matilda looked around and then spoke up. "I wanted to try it," she said. "I never understood why our Terry loved being a part of his football team. He'd come home covered in mud, cuts and bruises, devastated after a humiliating six nil defeat. Then the next Saturday, he'd wake up excited to do the whole thing all over again. I never understood it. I wanted to experience what he loved so much. I understand it now. I was curious at first, that's why I answered the advert. Now I'm here because I'm a part of something, the Allsorts."

Martha spoke up next. "I joined because I wanted to do something for the war effort. I just deliver the telegrams. No one wants to see me knocking on their door. I thought if we were raising money for charity, I could contribute more. As you know, I wasn't going to play at all today, not after last time, but I think I was only upset because it meant something to me, because I felt like I let you all down. I didn't want to do that again. This team gives me something to believe in, something to fight for, I suppose. Whether we win or lose, we should be proud of that if nothing else."

"We can still win this," Ned said, sensing that

the mood was dipping towards an acceptance of defeat. "It isn't over yet."

"Why did you answer the advert, Ned?" Martha asked.

"I didn't answer the advert. I was always going to play. Kit is my oldest friend." She paused and looked round at the team. "I never had a family. I don't have anyone in the stands cheering me on. Everyone who means anything to me is on the pitch. I always wondered what it would be like. To have a group of people I can rely on, no matter what. Now I know."

"Why are you here, Kit?" Miss Bamford asked.

"I suppose I thought I had something to prove. To show this town that I'm not the waste of space everyone thinks I am. You all know it was my brother Bernie's dream to win the cup, and he tried, he really tried. I felt it was my job to finish what he started, to win the cup for him because he couldn't." I grabbed the loser's medal from under my jersey and clasped it in my hand. As I looked around at the rosy-cheeked, expectant faces of the Allsorts Football team, I realised that I'd been given a second chance.

"But it's more than that. For a minute back there, I thought I wouldn't be allowed to play, but now I can, I'm going to make the most of it." I leant forward and the others leant in around me. "I don't know what football means to you, but for me, it's the one thing that has always been there. Throughout everything, I've always had football. For ninety minutes nothing else matters, the whole world melts away. There's no war or work or bother. Without football, my life would be a miserable existence. Football makes sense when nothing else does." I paused, and we listened to the sound of the crowd on the terraces outside.

Miss Bamford cleared her throat. "Might I offer an observation?" I nodded and she stepped forward. "I know your reasons for playing. You've made that very clear. But I've been watching the match amongst the crowd and I can tell you that this team has a tremendous amount of support. The Carmody fans are all workers and families from Carmody Munitions, but The Allsorts fans are everyone else. And let me tell you, all those individuals singing together make quite some noise. We have supporters from all over town; shop workers, hatters, railway workers, soldiers, nurses, blacksmiths, servants, some men and lots of women. Everyone who never had a team to call their own until now. The Allsorts have captured their imagination, given them something to get behind, it brings them together, it's something that reminds them of better times, that gives them hope that better times will come again. In my opinion, whether you realised it or not, that's why you're all here today."

We looked at each other as we heard the click clack of the Carmody team's boots as they made their way back to the pitch. I stood, and the team gathered around me.

"The Carmody team might be better than us." I raised my hand to silence the objections. "They are, they train more, they have a strong squad of players to choose from, they have better kit, shinier boots and a belief that they can win because they always have. But we've got something they don't have."

"What's that?" Matilda asked.

"We have each other. We have fight. It means more to us. And to our supporters. Just listen to that." The girls looked towards the door. We could hear the chants and singing from the crowd. "Ned's right. This isn't over yet." There were smiles and nods of agreement. "We need to go out there and play for those people who have left their warm homes on Christmas day to stand in the freezing cold and cheer us on. We can do anything if we stick together. All of us; Ned and Martha, and

Matilda, and Claudie and Ivy and Lucy and Freda, Esther, Alice and Rachel and Miss Bamford." Miss Bamford smiled, happy to be included in the line up. "We're not just any old team, we're The Allsorts Football Team."

CHAPTER 38

Our first goal was an absolute belter. Martha passed the ball to Matilda, who tried to trap it under her foot the way I had shown her, but she missed the ball and it rolled into the path of one of the Carmody Munitionettes who was tying her shoelace. She looked up to see the ball rolling towards her, followed by several Allsorts players. She panicked, kicked the ball away from the goal, and it rolled out for a corner. This was our chance. I stood at the corner flag and raised my arm. My breathing was fast but steady. I shouted for the Allsorts to get into the goalmouth. When they were ready, I sent the ball flying in front of the goal. I watched everyone jump in unison as the ball flew over their heads. I had over hit it. But then, behind the heap of bodies, Ivy stood alone. Eyes on the ball, she leant backwards and made beautiful contact with her left foot. The ball flew powerfully past the stranded keeper and into the back of the net. A deafening cheer followed an astonished silence. The team surrounded Ivy, patting her on the back and clapping. One- two. We were back in the game.

Minutes after the restart, Carmody broke free and ran in front of our goal. Ned made a last second lunging tackle against Aggie, who screamed and fell to the floor. The crowd were on their feet demanding a penalty. Aggie hobbled after the referee, but he waved for play to continue. Esther, our keeper, didn't waste any time. She kicked the ball long, and we ran on the break. I received the ball on the wing and used everything I had ever learnt from reading the match reports in the papers and from the hours and hours I had spent in the park. A Carmody defender rushed in, but I side-stepped her and found myself one on one with the goalkeeper. I feigned a high kick and instead drove the ball low and straight over the line. Two- all with less than ten minutes to go. I ran into the net, picked up the ball and carried it back to the centre spot.

I waited for the referee to restart play. The Carmody manager shouted instructions to Aggie, who relayed the messages to the rest of her team. They were to attack, keep hold of the ball and not let us into their half. We would have to give it everything. To make matters worse, one of their players, who had been quiet all game, suddenly got a burst of energy. She was like a whirlwind, fast and nimble. Every time one of our players got a sniff of the ball, she bundled them out of the way. It was a single-handed effort. I watched on, screaming at our team to pass the ball. We had a proper fight on our hands.

Play went on. The clock ticked down. We expected the referee to blow the full time whistle any second. A restart resulted in the ball flying high and bouncing between the players, each side lofting it high towards the opposition net in the hope it might go in. The ball landed at my feet and I found myself unmarked. I pulled my leg back and struck the ball with all my might in the general direction of the goal; I wasn't far beyond the halfway line. The ball floated in the air, taking an age to reach its peak before dipping towards the posts. The Carmody goalie held her line, never taking her eyes off the ball. I ran after the ball along with everyone else, eyes skyward. It fell sharply and for a glorious second looked as if it would sail unopposed into the goal, but at the last moment it changed course and clattered into the crossbar. The Allsorts' supporters groaned.

After a scrappy few minutes, we found ourselves back in the Carmody goal mouth. Their star player ran out of steam and we left her behind. They had everyone upfront. Bodies on the line. In the scuffle, one of their defenders threw in a sliding tackle and knocked Matilda over with a crunch. Matilda stayed down. Every player wanted a say with the referee. But I stayed out of it. It was an ugly scene, but it excited the crowd. The referee saw the whole thing. This was Carmody all over. If they couldn't win fairly, they would fight dirty. By the time everyone had calmed down, the referee blew his whistle and pointed to the penalty spot. Martha picked up the ball.

"It's alright," she said. "I can take it."

I scanned the crowd, looking for Mum. I put my hand over Bernie's medal around my neck. If we were going to win this, we would do it the right way. I found Mum, and she nodded, telling me with a look that she believed I could do it. "No, I'm the captain," I said. "I'll take it." Martha handed me the ball, relief written all over her face.

The girls knew what to do. We had trained for this. They took their places outside the penalty area, ready to pounce on any rebounds. The Carmody players lined up, waiting to kick the ball away. Aggie walked past me.

"I feel like we've been here before," she said, smiling. She was right. We had. The same goal, the same spot, the same crowd of people willing me to fail. I looked at the goalkeeper, who clapped her hands and stared at me. I placed the ball on the spot. My mouth was dry. I felt my heart beating against my ears, my hands were numb. I stood alone on the pitch in silence. All the spectators dissolved, leaving the stand empty. The players drifted away. The goal mouth stood clear, unprotected. All I had to do was hit the ball. Kick it like I had a hundred thousand times before. But out of nowhere, I couldn't remember how. All the thoughts crowded in on me. What if I missed? What if I slipped? What if I lost my temper and got sent off? What if mine was the last kick of the match? What if after all our hard work I let everyone down? What if…?

"What if you score?" It was Bernie's voice. "It's

just you, the ball, and the back of the net. Just shoot," he said. "You can do this, Kit Bracken."

I closed my eyes and imagined kicking the ball right into the corner of the goalmouth. If I picked my spot, I couldn't miss. I struck the ball with the right amount of power and lift. It sailed between the posts, brushed the fingertips of the outstretched goalkeeper, and swooshed into the net. Goal! Three- two. The referee blew his whistle before the ball had even stopped moving.

It was over. Final score three- two to the Allsorts.

My team mates ran in to me, hugging and cheering with delight and disbelief. I looked up at the stand. Mum was clapping, crying and laughing all at the same time.

Aggie Longstaff came over to shake my hand. "Well played," she said through her disappointment. "We'll get you next time though."

I stepped forward with my friends to accept the trophy. Of course, I had seen it close up once before. But this time, it wasn't a worthless piece of tin. As I put my hands on it, a tingling sensation ran through my fingers, as if it was charged with electricity. The hairs on my neck prickled. This time, I understood why it meant so much. My teammates crowded around, and we raised the trophy as one.

We are the Allsorts Football Team, winners of the Viaduct Cup.

Join the mailing list at www.nicclare.com to download a
FREE copy of 'The Munitionette- Aggie's story'.

Aggie Longstaff is the captain of the Carmody Munitionettes football team. She is popular and talented and she knows it.

The team work in the munitions factory, exposed to toxic chemicals, noise and filth. Everyone must play their part in the war effort- everyone. Aggie is quite prepared to hand out white feathers to those who shirk their duty.

A grudge match against old rival Kit Bracken and her new team of Allsorts gives Aggie the chance to show what she is made of.

But when tragedy strikes, Aggie learns that there are always two sides to every story…

Did you enjoy Kit's story?

Ivy's story is available now.

'The Allsorts FC Series Book Two: The Search'

The Allsorts football team need all their best players on the pitch. But star striker Ivy Winstanley finds her loyalties divided.

When a telegram arrives with terrible news from the trenches of the Great War, she leaves everything behind in a search for answers.

She joins the 'Missing and Wounded Bureau,' who work to give comfort to worried relatives.

But in her journey towards the front line, Ivy finds more than just answers…

THE SEARCH

Chapter 1

I trapped the ball underneath my right boot and looked up as a defender rushed in at me. I had to act fast, so I stepped to my left, tapped the ball gently to stop it and then, as if I had all the time in the world, I drew my leg back and chipped the ball over the Carmody team's defence. I knew instantly that it was going all the way. The ball brushed the goalkeeper's fingertips as she stretched, but she could only watch as it burst into the back of the net. I think I might have gone deaf for a second, because the sound of the crowd roaring almost burst my eardrums. Well, it felt that way to me. My team mates rushed in to celebrate. To score like that for your team is... well, it makes the hairs on the back of my neck stand up to remember it. I never dreamt of playing football. To be honest, I never even knew girls could play football, but the world is changing, the war has seen to that. For the rest of the match I kept running it over and over in my head. I couldn't keep the smile from my face. I wasn't to know then that the best day of my life was about to become the worst.

As we sat in the changing room with our trophy, reliving every kick and tackle, Miss Bamford our manager came in.

"Very well done girls. I knew you could do it. You should have seen the look on Lord Carmody's face when they blew the final whistle." Her cheeks were flushed like ours even though she hadn't been running on the pitch for ninety minutes.

Kit handed over the trophy. "Here, this is as much yours as it is ours." Miss Bamford held it out in front of her and shook her head in disbelief.

"You'd better remember this feeling," she said. "I've just met a chap from the Football Association and we've been entered into the National League Cup competition. This is just the beginning for the Allsorts."

As the singing started, I saw my little sister

Maud hovering by the door. She didn't have to say anything. I could tell by the look on her face.

"There's been a telegram, Ivy," she said. I took her hand, and we ran....

To buy the book and continue reading 'The Search' visit www.nicclare.com

Printed in Great Britain
by Amazon

17502336R00128